Haunted Summer

By Anne Edwards

The Survivors

Miklos Alexandrovitch Is Missing

Shadow of a Lion

Haunted Summer

Haunted Summer

by Anne Edwards

Coward, McCann & Geoghegan, Inc.
New York

Shelley, Percy Bysshe — Fiction
Shelley, Mary Wallstonecraft Godwin — Fiction
Byron, George Gordon Noel Byron, 6th baron —
    Fiction

For Vera Caspary

To whom this book
is most beholden

From far across the sea, Love,
I hear a wild lament,
By Echo's voice for thee, Love,
From Ocean's caverns sent.

MARY SHELLEY

Contents

Preface

Shelley once wrote in a letter to me that "the curse of this life is that what we have once known we cannot cease to know." He was right, yet, one may cease to remember; I have irrefutable evidence of that.

I had believed no moment that I had lived whilst Shelley and I shared a life together would ever be forgot. I have, in fact, endured the years since his death by devoting myself to the copying, editing and publication of all his work, and to the writing of notes to all his poems, that the world may understand the genius and the gentleness of the man as well as the circumstance in which the work was composed. I know of no greater genius who could have produced the weight of beauty that Shelley did. Yet, the time did come only this last summer, when no more remained for me to do on Shelley's behalf.

It was then that I took all his letters to me and all our entries into our journal and read them with the thought that I might embark upon the writing of an autobiography and while lost in the recall of those hours shared, discovered a packet of letters I had once dearly known and had forgot, and a grievous gap in the journal that we had apparently desired to remove (the pages encompassing over ten weeks were torn out and destroyed) but which memory had never permitted me to cease knowing.

All through the haunted summer that followed I turned my thoughts to those ten weeks when I was young and Shelley with me, and we lived for a time in the close company of Lord Byron, and with a young physician named Polidori and my step-sister Claire. The decision to remove those pages from my journal was made because Shelley and I feared infringement on the lives of our companions if the entries were ever inadvertently discovered and made public. Claire and I remain, however, and—however painful—the only living members of that quintet. And Claire, who has been the bane of my life since I was three, sees me no more, and is no longer cognizant of rational life.

The absent pages in the record of Shelley and my life together haunted me. I began to make notes and then found I was attempting to reconstruct the days almost entirely. I became torn to pieces by memory, but by the close of the summer what follows had been set down upon paper.

Whatever ghosts exist, whether the beloved dead make a portion of this company, I dare not guess. And yet, surely, on such an evening as this when one's hand rests upon such a record of joy and sorrow now past and when memory has numbed sensibility, and there is an atmosphere so hushed, so soft, that living spirits seem gathered round, credence may be given.

Quanto bene mi rammento, in questa medesima stagione i pensieri, i sentimenti del mio cuore! Allora cominciai Frankenstein. Allora sola col mio Bene fui felice. Allora le nuvole furono spinte dal furioso vento davanti dalla luna, nuvole magnifiche, che in forme grandiose e bianche parevano stabili quanto le montagne e sotta la tirannia del vento si mostravano piu fragili che un velo di seta minutissima, scendeva allor la pioggia, gli albori si spogliavanio. Antunno bello fosti allora ed ora bello terribile, malinconico ci sei, ed io, dove sono?*

Mary Shelley
Chester Square, London
25 October 1850

(Translation: How well do I remember, in this same season, the thoughts, the feelings of my heart. Then I began *Frankenstein.* Then, alone with my Beloved, I was happy. Then the clouds were driven by the furious wind before the moon—magnificent clouds, which, grand and white, seemed as stable as the mountains, and under the tryanny of the wind appeared more fragile than a veil of finest silk. Came then the rain, despoiling the trees. Autumn, you were beautiful then, and now you are beautiful, terrible, and melancholy—and I, where am I?)

Prologue

I come to St. Pancras' graveyard often. Especially after the midnight chimes. I am alone then. The mourners are gone, the gravediggers done with their task and the dead left to their eternal solitude. I do not mean to intrude upon their private world, but spirits rest there who were once a part of mine.

Memory is now the only wick my candle has. All I loved have long since gone—father, mother, sister, friend, husband, child—all made as it were a team that conducted me here and then left me alone to fulfill my task. So be it. I question not the dead, but I visit them—their spirits might entreat me.

A gauzy veil has crossed the moon. The night is cold and restless. It is autumn and warm breezes are only distant memory. Truth, *he* was not buried here among these baroque headstones and ancient trees, the Gothic arches of St. Pancras just beyond. No, Shelley rests beneath the blue sky of Rome. But his spirit hovers over me wherever I may be.

Here by my mother's tomb, we once sat enfolded in each other's arms. It was past midnight then, as now. Spring had brought us that far and the sands of summer were still without imprint.

If I could but see my own lean, golden Shelley once more, his waving hair to his shoulders, his intelligent face, the sensitive mouth, the inquisitive eyes and the very livingness of his touch. And myself, a girl still, younger than even Shelley's twenty-two years—nineteen only—golden-headed, pale-faced, large hazel, hopeful eyes.

I can hear the clock in St. Pancras' church strike one and recall the awesome silence that follows. I awake first and then Shelley stirs. He is turned away from me, his eyes closed. The wind has stilled, the veil is lifting. A shiver passes through me. All seems unreal, until he wakes drowsily and takes me in his arms. Until we kiss. And then we rise up from the damp grass at the foot of the tomb and holding hands, walk through the silent graveyard. Here a willow dips low, and there cut daisies droop at the foot of a grave. We draw apart and interlocking our hands over our heads, as in a game of London Bridge, pass over graves still too young to bear a legend. We laugh! Not out of irreverence but communion. Oh, but we would live, live, live—Shelley and his own Mary! And then we break apart and dodge between the graves until we reach the high, grey walls that guard the marble fields.

Then we grow silent, our laughter contained as we

walk through the nighttime shadows of London, hardly breathing when a night watchman passes by—side by side, unafraid, confident the dead are behind us forever. Oh, my beloved Shelley, how often during those happy days I thought how superiorly gifted I had been in being united to one to whom I could unveil myself and who could understand me.

But now no eye answers mine; my voice can with none assume its natural modulation. Yet standing here this night, I seem to see you well. I would give worlds to sit, my eyes closed, listening to you speak once again. I was once selected for happiness—let the memory of that content me. You pass by an old ruined house in a desolate lane and heed it not. But if you hear that house is haunted by a wild and beautiful spirit, it acquires an interest and a beauty of its own.

So other summers will come and go. Leaves you never saw will shadow the grounds and flowers you never beheld will star it, the grass will be of another growth and the birds sing a new song, and the aged earth date with a new number. But that summer when we left England, taking Claire and all our expectations with us to Switzerland, like children parading to a Christmas village— that summer lingers on like bars of a known air and seems to be a wind rousing from its depths every deepseated emotion of my heart.

Haunted Summer

1

After nine frantic days of travelling, we reached Switzerland by nightfall of the tenth. We had succeeded in our elopement. Yet what shadows followed us in the wind! We had known and loved each other for two years, since I was seventeen and Shelley hardly twenty.

We had met in my own home on Skinner Street. My father was William Godwin, revolutionary, writer, publisher, whose great work *Political Justice* influenced the intellect of a youth of ardent temperament and aspiring moral views. He was the disciple of the New School and our house on Skinner Street had, since my first remembrances, drawn young men of enthusiastic reverence. Such was Shelley, for the revolutionary spirit burned deeply within him. He was, at the time, writing political pamphlets which my father published and was giving the majority of his allowance from his share of his family estate to my father's revolutionary cause.

I cannot know what Shelley felt upon first seeing me, but I knew that very instant that my life had just been touched by genius. There was between us the volcanic forces of the erotic and the intellectual that made our final union predestined. It was, therefore, for both of us, a tragedy that Shelley was already wed.

Harriet . . . Shelley's wife . . . responsible for so many of our problems and yet, if Harriet had been other than what she was, perhaps there would have been no cause for the growth of the wonderful spirit of understanding that soon existed between Shelley and myself.

It is the darkest enigma that my father was so against our liaison from the start. For my mother had been Mary Wollstonecraft, famous for her *Vindication of the Rights of Woman*, staunch believer in free love. They say she only married my father, mere weeks before my birth, because on reflection she felt she only had the right to live her own life according to her rules and that inflicting illegitimacy on me was not moral. And having given birth to my older half-sister Fanny in that manner, she had already seen the blind hand of intolerance set to work. She died when I was only twelve days old, but sometimes I feel her spirit lives within me. It is to my mother's tomb I went for consolation as a girl, and it was by her grave marker that Shelley and I would meet and love. Strange though that may seem, it never seemed strange to Shelley or myself.

No, Father's fury at our affair was never based on moral grounds, but on the shifting sands of Shelley's fortunes after our affair became scandal to all London.

For Harriet vindictively, extravagantly, and carelessly ran up enormous debts, and Shelley's father, outraged at our love, discontinued Shelley's allowance. Shelley had written two romantic novels and the infamous *Queen Mab*, but the latter's atheistic philosophy had held the printing down to 250 copies, and a private printing at that! He was not able to survive and support Harriet and their two children on his writing, nor (and this, of course, was my father's first concern) support the causes of political justice.

My father turned on us, the bailiffs pursued us tirelessly, and Shelley was in danger of arrest due both to debts and his political pamphlets. All of which makes our elopement seem more like an escape. And, indeed, perhaps that is what it truly was. Certainly, it was only when we reached Switzerland that I first felt safe.

We had taken Claire with us, a fact that had enraged my step-mother, now left with only Fanny to help her at home. Claire, unbalanced, excitable, sometimes hysterical . . . Claire! How could we take her along and, yet, how could we have left her behind? Though she had not confided in us, Shelley and I both were certain she was pregnant and was suffering severely with her secret. She begged us to take her, her violet eyes pleading — such great bruises in so small a pale, delicate face. It was unthinkable for us to refuse her. But it was only as we travelled from France to Switzerland that we were aware that our destination, Geneva, had been Claire's desire, not our own. We speculated that whoever Claire's mysterious lover might be, she had reason to believe he could be found there. He might be overjoyed at being united with Claire and accept full responsibility for her and the child, but we had to face the alternative—that he could remain forever elusive, in which case Shelley would have to bear the full burden, and he with present resources to support us all only till summer's end!

In spite of all this, my happiness was boundless as our coach passed onto Swiss soil and we neared our destination. The horned moon hung in the light of a sunset that threw a glow of unusual depth of redness above the piney mountains and the dark, deep valleys. Beyond us, hill after hill extended its craggy outline before the other, and far behind all, towering above every feature of the scene, the snowy Alps, looking like those accumulated clouds of dazzling white that arrange themselves on the horizon in summer.

We stopped at an inn at the foot of Montanvert. Had our day's journey not been so exhausting, we might have continued on, for the place was dark and narrow-windowed and there was in every room the scent of decay. After a meagre meal, we were led to our rooms by a stooped man, ancient but hard, the candle held too low to light the shadows that hung about our heads.

Claire was directly across the corridor from us. She nervously said good night and we stood waiting until she was safely inside. Our room was most depressing. It was dark and shuttered. An old spinet sat in one corner, but several of its keys were missing, making it seem to match the ancient's smile. There was a case of stuffed birds in another corner, a sight I could not bear to look on. Our guide left us candles but we did not light them and instead opened the shuttered windows wide and let in the fingers of night light from the moonlit midnight sky.

We were alone.

The bed was large and comfortable and faced the windows and Shelley held me in his arms and we looked out into the night. Neither of us could sleep, but neither could we speak. The silence breathed like a warm wind about us, more comfort than the softest down. Then, moments later, or perhaps it was longer, for time had lost its memory, there was a timid tapping at the door. Shelley rose to see who it might be and Claire entered almost before he bid her to do so. She came to the foot of my bed and stood pale-faced, eyes wide and frightened.

"What is it, Claire?" I asked as I got out of the bed and went to her and placed my arm about her shoulders. She was trembling and dressed only in a nightdress.

"There are rats," she whimpered. "They came and put their cold paws on my face."

"It must have been a bad dream," I assured her.

"No. *No!* There were rats. Rats with cold paws, and they walked upon my face. I *will not go back*," she cried.

I guided her to the side of the bed and Shelley gave us room and she rested with us. I held her in my arms as Shelley slept beside me, and I stroked her hair until at last she had fallen into an exhausted sleep. She looked like a small frightened child and, indeed, I realized with a start that at a scant eighteen, she was hardly more. Nightmares such as the rats had plagued Claire since we left England, but she had had such dreams when we were children and I had comforted her then, as I did this night.

By morning she seem refreshed and the wild dream of the night faded with the moon. She chattered endlessly as we continued on and up Montanvert and was less affected than I at the desolation of this mountain; the

:[25]:

trees in many places torn away by avalanches, some half leaning over others and intermingled with stones. And to add to the eerie atmosphere it began to rain almost as soon as we left the inn. When we had ascended considerably, we turned to look on the scene. A dense white mist covered the vale, and tops of scattered pines peeping above were the only objects that presented themselves.

We reached the top by twelve. No wonder it is called *le Mer de Glace.* It must be the most forsaken place in the world. Iced mountains surround it, no vegetation appears except on the place from which we viewed the scene, and the air is very cold. Yet, there were rhododendron and *Roses des Alpes* growing in great profusion where we stood.

Claire's face was red with cold and her eyes watery; she kept blowing into cupped hands to warm herself.

"Shall we go?" Shelley asked.

"No, I like the cold," she insisted. Then she laughed. "Papa says it's good to suffer. That it makes a person rise to the best in him."

Still, Shelley hurried the guide along and we were shortly on our way, huge pines rising beside us, rising in clumps from the white wilderness, looking strange in the twilight while the wide silence of the snow desert was broken only by the distant calls of labouring mountaineers.

But soon the evening became calm and beautiful and the horses went fast and the plain opened before us and the deep blue waters of Lake Leman glistened beneath a clear, crisp night sky, dazzled by the brilliance of the stars, looking close enough to touch. We were silent most of the journey. Occasionally Shelley would take my hand in his to reassure me, for he could see that my thoughts were turbulent—a confusion of what we had left behind us and the small fears of what might lie ahead.

The road we were on ran by the side of the lake, becoming narrower as we continued on. Shelley suggested stopping at a small inn by the shore but Claire insisted we continue on to Sêcheron where she had heard of a fashionable inn and where she was sure we could find lodgings.

"It might be a bit too grand for our pockets," Shelley warned.

"Oh, but Shelley," Claire persisted, "one night. Imagine! They say *all* the most exciting people stop there." Tears rimmed her eyes. "I am so weary of dirty boats and rats, and cold rooms, and hard beds. It has been ten days. Please, Shelley?"

"Sêcheron, it is," he replied.

We rode on with the black sides of Jura to one side of us and the white summit of Mont Blanc ahead and by the time we arrived at Sêcheron, which was past nine, we were too exhilarated by the beauty of the lake, the night, the mountains to be exhausted. Too filled with a sense of our own youth and daring and love to be anything but happy. And as we entered the elegant foyer of Dejean's Hôtel de l'Angleterre, none of us truly gave any thought to the plight we were in. There we were—Shelley at twenty-three, me in my nineteenth year and Claire in her eighteenth. She, carrying a bastard child, and Shelley and I fugitives from our own country, a deserted wife, irate parents and the law, and with very little money in our pockets.

Claire was the first to enter the hotel, the first to approach the reception desk. As I stood in the entrance, waiting for Shelley to join us after tending to the coach and our baggage, I observed her studying the hotel register. She asked the clerk something in French, very low, I could not hear her words at all, but he answered her quite clearly and in English.

"No, the English Lord and his friend have not arrived," he said.

"Friend?" Claire asked, her hand nervously tucking stray ends of blond hair into the bun at her neck.

But Shelley came in then and Claire moved quickly away from the desk. All the time that Shelley was making our accommodations, Claire stood in the large bay window that overlooked the courtyard entrance. There was the answer then! Claire was in love with an English Lord whom she was hoping to meet at this hotel and she had obviously not informed him she would be arriving for there had been no message waiting for her.

There was to be none for several days, but the hotel was such a joy that Shelley agreed readily to our remaining. We hired a boat and every evening about six o'clock we would sail on the lake. Unlike the Channel crossing just past, the tossing of our little boat on Lake Leman raised my spirits and filled us all with an unusual hilarity. Some of my fears were beginning to diminish as Shelley and I were drawn closer by our mutual escape from England and by the severing of our past ties.

It was on a Saturday night several days after our arrival and we had just returned from one of our moonlight rides when Claire's mysterious Lord finally appeared.

He arrived in a lavish coach that was an exact copy of

drawings I had seen of Napoleon's imperial carriage. It was tremendous in size and contained a *lit de repos* and a library. But there were two other coaches as well, a bevy of manservants and what seemed to be endless cases and trunks and a curious ménage of animals.

His own coachman helped him from his carriage. He was a young man, certainly not yet thirty, short of stature and yet very striking. He was dressed elegantly, smoked a small cigar and carried a gold-handled cane. He was lame and wore a built-up boot, and on his shoulder perched a sharp-eyed and chattering monkey. He had one of those exceptional faces that one never could forget, having seen it only once. Darkly handsome, brooding eyes, wide sensuous mouth—a mixture of arrogance and vulnerability, intensity and flamboyance, intelligence and devil-may-care. Claire's mysterious Lord, the father of her unborn child, was, incredibly, George Gordon—*Lord Byron*.

His friend hovered possessively about him. From the very first moment I set eyes on John William Polidori, flourishing his black cape grandly, his handsome, dark Italian face courting an arrogant smile, I distrusted him. He carried a small black case and refused to release it to the servants.

"God! I am exhausted," Lord Byron told him. "See to the baggage for me, Poli."

Lord Byron strode across the courtyard to be greeted by the proprietor who ushered him inside with a good deal of scraping and bowing.

I had not been prepared for the celebrity of Claire's lover. For Lord Byron was at the time England's most famous poet. He was also England's greatest scandal,

:[29]:

known for his sexual exploits and his outrageous behaviour in society. He had been involved in an incestuous relationship with his sister, Augusta, the story went, and had fathered her child, Medora, whilst married to another. Politically, he had been a revolutionary as Shelley had. And in April, just a short time before we left England, he, too, had been forced to leave and was now an exile and, as we were, homeless and in search of home.

Later, Claire told me how she had met Lord Byron. Knowing him to be an influence at Drury Lane and wanting so to be an actress, she had gathered all her courage and called on him without so much as a note of introduction. I had been so involved in Shelley's and my own plight, that I had not been as aware as I should have of Claire's unhappy state after this meeting and those that followed. It was easy enough to understand how Claire, unhappy, unknown, of little experience, a girl in her eighteenth year, could have been blinded by Lord Byron's attentions. To feel herself beloved by the most extraordinary genius, the most romantic and most famous man in England who had a lacerated heart to which she might bring healing, must have been heady indeed. No, it was not strange at all that a girl like Claire, excitable, lacking judgment, brooding and silently rebellious against our father, and whose intellect, like my own, had been imbued with the social doctrines of revolutionary thinkers, should have been whirled out of her regular orbit by such a force as Lord Byron. It was also understandable now why Claire had felt a need to keep this great man and event in her life secret. She was not yet confident of the depth of her lover's passion.

:[30]:

Claire stood across the entire expanse of the huge reception room, her shawl drawn tightly around her shoulders, as Lord Byron entered. My heart seemed to stop for a moment as I saw that he was not only surprised but obviously displeased to see her. He turned away instantly without greeting her and became immediately preoccupied with the business of signing the register. When he had put the pen down, the proprietor cleared his throat nervously.

"Your address, your Lordship?" he inquired.

"At present, here."

"I beg your indulgence, your Lordship, but the authorities . . . . "

"Damn the authorities!"

"May I write . . . England . . . your Lordship?"

"As you please!" He began to move away from the desk.

"And your age, your Lordship?" the proprietor called after him.

"My age?" Lord Byron laughed sharply and then, looking directly at Claire, said, "at this moment one hundred!"

Claire seemed paralyzed. A servant led his Lordship across the room. They would have to pass her to reach the stairway. As they did, Claire stepped forward and between them, freeing the servant to pass on but barring Lord Byron's path. Her hand loosened its hold on her shawl and she rested it on his arm. There was a tense and yet curiously tender moment. For an instant their eyes met and something of very strong emotion passed between them. Then he drew away and Claire's hand fell limply and she quickly grasped her shawl to her again.

:[31]:

"It was indiscreet of me to tell you where I would be, but it was unpardonable of you to be here!" he said, his voice cold, his glance now steel.

Claire flinched as though he had struck her. "And unforgivable for you to treat me thus, Milord . . . " she snapped back. Her body stiffened but as he went to pass her, her voice grew softer and her eyes misty, " . . . when not so long ago . . ." Her voice trembled and Lord Byron for one brief moment leaned towards her as if for support, then he braced himself again.

"You should listen to rumour. It has me a violent man," he said, his voice filled more with wry humour than displeasure.

"I could report you a tender one," Claire replied with a hint of pride in her voice.

His friend approached at just that moment. "Dr. Polidori," said Byron, introducing him.

"Milord's companion," Dr. Polidori smiled.

"My private physican," Lord Byron added.

"You have been ill, Milord?" Claire asked with some concern.

"At this moment simply distressed."

"I know the hour, but I must have a word with you."

"Can it not wait?"

Her answering glance seemed to assure him it could not.

Lord Byron went before Claire, but he led her to his chambers and then closed the door. His physician, the young man with the foreign sounding name of Polidori, stood in the corridor outside, his face dark with anger.

I learned shortly afterwards that Polidori's father was Italian and his mother English. He had been endowed with the best features of both: large, deep, dark, flashing eyes beneath heavy brows, an aquiline nose and slender aristocratic nostrils, wide sensuous mouth, slow to smile, even white teeth, a square cleft chin and broad, high forehead, thick dark hair dressed impeccably, ivory-skinned, broad of stature, a grace of movement, and a charmingly accented voice—that was Polidori—and I could not deny his attractiveness. Yet there was something so loathsome about him that as I stood there, my flesh crawled. He was an evil man, I was certain of it. Certain as well, that a relationship of an exceedingly dark nature existed between him and Lord Byron.

2

I shall, of course, never know what occurred between Claire and Lord Byron at that first meeting in Swit zerland. Claire never spoke of it, and I could not bring myself to ask. It was enough to see her calm and seemingly happy.

She came to our room extremely early the next day. She was dressed in her best frock and her hair was curled provocatively about her face.

"You were surprised," she preened. "Now admit it, you were *pleased*. And so is he. 'Shelley, what luck!' he said," Claire was imitating Lord Byron's curious deep-throated voice, "and he was surprised and pleased too! He says you are a great poet, Shelley, and he was absolutely gloating when I told him how you had left England as he did. 'Quite right!' he said, as though you were blood brothers!"

She danced across the room and flopped down at the foot of the bed. "We are having lunch together. I promised him . . . I mean, *all* of us. Of course, no one dares talk to him. Women *faint* if he speaks to them." She fluttered her hand in mockery before her face and lowered her eyes. "He is considered Mephistophelian," she leaned forward and winked, "terribly wicked, you know."

"I have heard," I agreed.

Shelley was already out of bed and preparing to dress.

Claire leaned in very close to me and whispered, "They will like each other. I always knew they would." Then as she straightened, "I love him very much, Mary. You do approve?"

"I could certainly only approve of anyone who seems to make you so happy."

We laughed as she went out, but a spirit of gaiety now pervaded our little triangle, and I was happier than I had been in a long while.

Shelley and Lord Byron were naturally and inevitably drawn together. Both were poets; both were children of the Revolution, the one representing its temper of indignant revolt, the other, its wild-eyed hopes. Both had warred against the laws of society and were rebels under the ban. Lord Byron (or Albé as we all soon called him, a name drawn from his fondness for telling stories of his exploits years before with the Albanian armies) was a man who exerted his genius with such force as to overpower us all at times. He was an exceedingly interesting person, and yet, even my Shelley recognized that he was slave to the vilest and most vulgar prejudices and shared my presentiments that he was as mad as the winds. Yes, Albé was a consummate genius, but it was his weakness to be proud. Shelley, on the other hand, was a far less domineering power, far more the speculator and dreamer. In this very fact rested his own strength, for his faith was always in ideas which had a great future before them, and his dreams were of how good could be made superior to the evil in this world.

I shall always hold the image in my mind of those two magnetic forces brought together for the first time. Sensitive Shelley, his slender frame seeming overcharged with the weight of life, his soul appearing rather to inhabit his body than to unite with it. Excellent Shelley, loving all, beloved by all, prone to wander by himself in nature with a book as his only companion, subject to heights few others could reach and depths to which most could not or would not descend. And Lord Byron, haughty, writhing beneath an injury he seemed unable to revenge. Reckless, proud, the dark hero of slanderous tongues—gay, ruthless, brilliant Lord Byron turning to sport every word that was uttered. The attraction between these two men was natural. Yet, their immediate and warm bond of friendship somehow surprised me.

Claire seemed quite content, however, that Albé and Shelley should be friends. I daresay it was what she had hoped for all along, as that friendship made us a close group (though I am certain she would have preferred the closer intimacy of a *foursome*; Polidori's presence excluded such a possibility as he was always in attendance). Claire had still not discussed her impending motherhood with either Shelley or myself and I did not press for such a discussion, as I felt she first needed a sound indication of Albé's position in the matter. Then, too, I knew Polidori disturbed her, as he did Shelley and myself. Or perhaps, to be more honest, it was Albé's dependence on Polidori that was disturbing. We knew that Albé was experimenting with opium and laudanum and that Polidori supplied these drugs. We knew also that Albé had once, when a young man at Harrow, had a scandalous relationship with another male student, which had caused his being sent down.

From the moment Albé's eyes met mine, I was aware a challenge had been extended. At the time I did not take it personally. One could immediately sense that Albé was not a man, no matter how liberal and nonconformist his views, to give a woman equal standing, and from our first meeting he came to accept that I was a woman who would never compromise at less.

"*Mistress Mary*," his voice curled sarcastically about the words, "may I help you into the coach?" And this only moments after we had been introduced and before embarking for our elegant lunch!

I ignored his outstretched hand, stepped in by my own aid and settled back to wait for the others to join me, but I could hear Shelley say, "I am afraid Mary objects to being called mistress."

"Even by you?" Albé inquired sharply.

"Mary, my love, my dearest friend, my life partner. But *Mistress Mary*, never," Shelley laughed.

"Call herself what she may, I find that a mistress never is, nor can ever be—a friend. For while you agree, you are lovers. And, when it is over, anything but friends. Now, Shelley, two mistresses. *Ah!* Well, that is quite another matter! Two or more are manageable by division."

Albé laughed at his own words and then helped Claire into the coach, as Shelley and he joined us.

"Are you planning eventually to return to England?" he asked Shelley.

"I suppose I must," Shelley smiled distantly. "And you?"

"Return to England? For what purpose? I hope to hell and damnation that even my bones do not become meal for English worms. I am no martyr, Shelley, and altars are stained with blood and polluted with gold!"

Shelley's eyes shone with fond memory. "I am afraid it will always be my England—with its greyer skies, its fields, its green lanes, its hills and streams—ties which, until I become utterly senseless, can never be broken asunder."

Albé sat back and glared at us all, his intense dark eyes studying the sun on Claire's face, the smile on Shelley's, the anticipation on Polidori's and the defiance on my own.

"Is there anything in the future," he commented finally, "that can possibly console us for not always being young, Shelley? Truly, only the young can accomplish the impossible."

At that moment I was certain he spoke the truth.

Albé loved the water as we all did, and so he bought a boat, keeled and clinker-built, and early in the evenings we would embark, often to Albé's delight, having to struggle against the tide and wind. As often, we would land for a walk and he would loiter behind, lazily trailing his swordstick after him. Sometimes, he would lie down at the bottom of the boat and gaze up at heaven, which he swore he would never enter.

For those few evening hours in our small boat, we could live between two wonderful worlds, the waters beneath, the heavens overhead, but once back at the hotel, reality would set in. Albé was Albé no more. He was the scandalous Lord Byron. Twice on an evening ride by himself, he was waylaid and accused of corrupting all *grisettes* in the Rue Basse. He believed these townspeople looked upon him as a man-monster, somebody possessed. "When I walk through the reception of this hotel," he said, "ladies faint and others look at me as though *His Satanic Majesty* had just been among them!" Then scowling in his most demonaic manner, he vowed to find himself a cloistered villa, unapproachable and without access to prying eyes.

We had secured a small, inexpensive cottage, the Campagne Chapuis, near Cologny, on the opposite side of the lake. The cottage was separated from the water's edge by a small garden overgrown by trees and was directly below and only a few minutes' walk from a larger house, the Villa Diodati, where Milton, returning from Italy in 1639, had visited his friend Dr. John Diodati, the Genevan professor of theology. A vineyard lay between the villa and our own cottage, with a narrow winding lane leading from the upper house to the terrace and a little harbour where we kept our small boat at her mooring. The two houses and the harbour were almost entirely hidden from the road and made private by a grove of trees, almost like two birds' nests among a forest of leaves. From windows of both houses Jura could be seen, behind whose range the sun sank, darkness winging onward along the valleys, but the Alps beyond glowing and roseate in the brilliance of the sunset.

It was not a difficult task to convince Albé to let the larger house, the Villa Diodati.

From that time we saw no one in Geneva and seldom even ventured into the village, sending Polidori whenever anything was required. We sailed on the lake most evenings, dined late and together remained awake until early morning talking, forever talking!

One night we enjoyed a finer storm than I had ever before beheld. The lake was lit up, the pines on Jura made visible, and all the scene illuminated for an instant, when a pitchy blackness succeeded and the thunder came in frightful bursts over our heads.

We had all gone up to Diodati rather early in the evening to watch the coming of the storm. Albé was working on the Third Canto of *Childe Harold* and Claire was in the habit of copying his work for him and often spent late afternoons with him at Diodati. This day we joined her. The sky was dark and threatening and grew black very quickly. There was something heavy, as if an unseen presence, about us. Albé's aviary of birds chittered, the cats bristled, the small bulldog growled from beneath a chair and the monkey clung to Albé's shoulder, crying pitifully.

We sat in the darkness and listened to the wild calls of the storm. Sound vibrated all about us. We were one with the storm, a part of the fury, the violence, the savagery. Finally, the winds fell, the sky turned a glowing violet and the air was indescribably alive.

Albé paced back and forth before the opened windows. In the distance we could hear the church clock at Cologny. It was ten o'clock. He turned to face us.

"We will take the boat out on the lake," he told us.

The monkey began to cry again and Albé scooped the small creature up in his arms and, holding him like a child against its mother's breast, stroked its shivering form.

Claire and I exchanged nervous glances, but Shelley and Polidori appeared enthusiastic about the idea, even though the sky was now black and there was cause to fear that the storm might erupt again. There was no moon and the path was in darkness. Polidori led, his eyes like a cat's, and also driven on by his incessant need to prove himself to Albé. The monkey would not quiet and Claire suggested turning back to return it to the house, but Albé would not hear of it.

In the darkness our boat looked like a burned-out hull. We lit the boat lantern and Polidori held the vessel steady as we climbed aboard. Then he got in and sat at the helm. We pulled away from the shore and steered the boat in the direction of Chillon. We had passed the castle many times and it had held a special fascination for us all, its rough-hewn rock façade extending as it did into Lake Leman, appearing at times to be the throne of some giant water god.

Shelley held me in his arms to shelter me from the chill wind. In the boat lantern's yellow glare I could see Polidori in his black cape and Albé, the monkey on his shoulder as he rowed. Claire was huddled on the bottom of the boat beneath a blanket to ward off the cold. Thankfully, the monkey had ceased its cries, but the wind was now quite unsettled and like a skittish cat, bristled past our ears.

We were now broadside of Chillon. It was almost totally dark within and without, except for the warning lanterns on the rock walls facing the water. It appeared to brood darkly at us—the water god displeased at the approach of strangers. Claire, who could not possibly see from the position she was in, sat up, and as the wind had spread Polidori's cape about him like a giant bat's wings blocking her view, made to stand to see around him and as she did, the boat tipped crazily.

What happened next, happened so quickly that I am not even certain I can recount it accurately. As well as I can remember, Shelley pulled Claire down and held us both steady as Albé lurched to one side to keep the boat from capsizing. But then, the monkey, squawking piteously, appeared to lose its grip on Albé's shoulder and catapulted into the water. We could hear it shrieking as it fought its fate. Before anyone of us could restrain him, Albé had stripped off his shirt and dived after the drowning animal. There was a steel box with supplies and candles and another lantern in it on the floor of the boat, and Shelley let go of us to unlock the box and prepare the lantern.

We could see Albé swimming towards shore with something in his arms. Shelley seized an oar and he and Polidori rowed as fast as was possible in so small a vessel on such turbulent waters.

We pulled to shore beneath the deep black shadows of Chillon's northern wall. The cold wind rendered candles useless. Shelley held the boat lantern high. Albé stood in its yellow glow, bending over the corpse of the monkey. As we approached, he straightened and turned, and without saying a word, took the cape from Polidori's shoulders and then went back to the corpse and covered it with the cape.

:[43]:

We stood in a circle around the dead animal's shroud, waiting as Albé gathered some sheltered, dry branches and placed them on top. Then, taking a match from Polidori, he set them alight. None of us could speak or move. The monkey's death seemed a strange foreboding. When the flames had died, Albe covered the hot ashes with damp earth. Then Claire helped him into his shirt, though in spite of the chill air, the wind and his wetness, he did not appear cold. In true fact, he had the appearance of a man with a slight fever.

Returning to Cologny by boat seemed foolhardy. We decided to rest at Chillon and if there was someone there to waken, ride back by horse or coach, if one was available, and then fetch our boat the next day. Chillon had not been inhabited for many years, but there were, as we understood it, a caretaker and guards.

That walk from the monkey's funeral pyre to the gates of Chillon is one I shall never forget. Since I was a girl in Scotland, I had been conscious of presentiments in which I not only could sense horror, but could in my mind, if only for a flash, envision the horror that would take place some time in the future. As the flames rose from the monkey's pyre, an image had appeared to me—Shelley, by the water, lifeless, a shroud not large enough to conceal his ghostly face—and then . . . *flames.*

It was now nearing midnight and there was no one at the gates, a fact which did not seem to deter Albé. We skirted the walls of the castle until we found one section that had decayed and not yet been repaired and was not too difficult to ascend by means of a human stepladder. So, with Polidori and Shelley to brace him, Albé scaled the wall and then came around and opened the gate for the rest of us.

We entered the courtyard, apparently not having awakened anyone. All was so dark, we assumed that Chillon must be deserted. The sky was empty of moon and stars as we crossed the moat and the rough, jagged cobblestoned courtyard by the light of a small boat lantern. The castle loomed dark and immense, and the only door we could find unlocked led to the dungeons. We lighted candles as we descended the thick stone stairway, none of us prepared for the awesomeness of the dungeon itself once we had fully descended. It was a long, narrow stone area, so long as to seem infinite, so high-ceilinged as to seem ceilingless. Huge Gothic columns rising and forming a vaulted stone ceiling divided the narrow room into two sharp archways—one side appearing the mirror image of the other, save for the thickly barred and deep carved windows on one wall. There were no shutters. The sound of swelling and angry waters echoed through the interior. It was cold and damp and the wind stirred the metal chains that hung from each stone pillar.

"It is so . . . eerie," Claire whispered.

She had huddled close to me and, I knew, needed the security of my nearness. Yet, it is difficult to explain, but I felt something quite different, almost spiritual. The same feeling I had always had at St. Pancras' graveyard by my mother's tomb. Strength slept here. Yet, it seemed awakened by our coming. Whatever horror had existed within these dark stone walls, it had been transcended by such a force of life that it had been harnessed into a new power. I drew away from Claire and, holding my single candle before me, walked beside the long row of stone pillars where the prisoners had once been chained. There is no explanation, really, but I stopped at one, and could not go a step farther.

I could hear Albé's now familiar step behind me, the harsh dragging of that one lame foot along the rough, uneven stone floor.

"There is a legend about a man being chained to that pillar for three long years," he told me. "He was known as the prisoner of Chillon. For three years he never went farther than the length of his chain."

He was beside me and, being not too much taller than I, almost on eye level. His dark eyes reflected the flames of our candles. For a long moment neither of us could speak, nor did we have to. Then he slipped away and called to the others. "Gather round! We shall make a game of this."

In a moment the others were by our side.

"Now, in a circle," he continued, "and everyone touch hands."

Shelley appeared unduly uncomfortable and I smiled encouragingly at him. Claire's hand grasped mine tightly. We had placed the candles on the stone floor in a ring before us. It was, I assume, Albé's intention to conduct some experiment in the supernatural. However, his plan was thwarted, for a tall, dark woman, looking like a Trojan woman, stood not ten feet from us. She held a lamp close to her, lighting her dark face and her huge, dark, heavy-browed eyes.

"Who are you?" she shouted and for the first time I

noted that she was trying to conceal a knife in her free hand by holding it between the folds of her skirt.

Albé immediately broke away and approached her. "Lord Byron, of Villa Diodati," he explained. "We were boating and met with an . . . accident."

The woman never moved. Her eyes studied us all. "There is a bell at the gate," she said, and now I detected a slight accent to her voice that was unmistakably Greek.

"We assumed Chillon was deserted at this hour," Albé told her.

"I am the caretaker. I never leave," she replied.

"Ah, but obviously you *do* sleep," Albé smiled, and his charm was not lost on the woman. "And obviously there are other beds where my companions and I might rest for the night." He crossed the few remaining feet to her side. I was sure he saw the knife, but he seemed unconcerned. His arm went about her shoulders.

"May I know your name?" he asked as he turned her away from us and began walking towards the stairway.

"Ianthe," she answered.

"Ianthe, so! and Ianthe it is!" Albé signaled us to follow and single-file we departed the dungeons behind him, our candles in hand, walking back up the steep stone stairway into the courtyard, crossing it to another door.

There was thunder rolling ominously across the skies, and as we entered the front door of Chillon, a blinding flash of white lightning obliterated the world outside.

3

The woman named Ianthe led us to our chambers through the darkened corridors of the deserted castle. She held her candle high as if in obeisance to the high, arching stone ceilings we passed beneath. It seemed a ritual act, one she might conduct nightly, chanting in her ancient tongue.

Albé, Polidori, and Claire were led to private chambers. At each one Ianthe would pause at the locked, thickly carved wooden door and without hesitation select the proper key from the crowded ring hanging from her sturdy waist by a metal chain. She would enter first, and, as we held no candles, we waited in darkness, able only to see through the open part of the door the light tracings from her candle as she circled the room making certain of its habitability. Then she would return to the corridor and beckon the guest chosen for that room to enter as she lighted the candles, and with a stiff nod of her head, left them inside and alone.

At the door of the fourth chamber, I took hold of Shelley's hand and as Ianthe swung its creaking portal open, stepped inside with Shelley. She was directly behind us. Her glance narrowed in disapproval as she turned to us.

"We are husband and wife," I told her.

Her glance went instantly to my ringless left hand, but she made no comment. Shelley and I stood awkwardly. The ancient guest room was musty from lack of air but dustless and impeccably preserved. The hearth was swept clean and there were no logs or kindling beside it. Yet, the room was not cold. We faced a bed starkly carved of white marble, the mattress covered in heavy lace and the canopy—marble as the posts, smooth and polished and faintly black-veined as though with spider's blood.

Ianthe stood by the side of the bed, her craggy face raised in pride. "The House of Savoy supplied Dukes for this castle since the twelfth century," she said, her voice as cold and unyielding as the marble bedpost she stroked possessively. Then her face mellowed and she drew her hand back close to her side. "There was once a brilliant era here in Chillon," she continued. "But never after the residence of the Dukes of Savoy. Chillon became a silent place then except for the sound of prisoners' cries and the rattle of their iron chains." She turned to us and a smile flickered across her face, barely seen, vanished before she spoke again. "For years—less than two decades ago—the castle was a prison and an arsenal. But I am helping it acquire a new life of its own." She crossed, unsmiling now, to the door. "On this rock, and within these great stones, the past has indeed returned. One need only reach out one's hand to touch it."

She left us standing there but soon returned with linens which she placed on a bench near the entrance to the room. It was apparent that she wanted it clearly understood that she would be servant to no intruders. Then she left us for the second time, now closing the door tightly so that all sound of her was immediately lost.

Shelley and I should have been over-wearied and wanting for sleep, but I could see that he shared my same excited state. Perhaps we were only intoxicated by the rarified air we breathed, but I believed instead it was due to the singular events of the evening and the bizarre and improbable turnings they had taken. We were tense and restless as Shelley opened the shutters whilst I placed fresh linen on the bed. A heavy rain was now falling and a soft wind carried its spray into the room. For several moments I stood beside Shelley in the cathedral-shaped window beneath an arch of praying hands and we looked out at the starless black night. Our room overlooked the lake shore, but though our ears were filled with the thrashing of the water as it beat against the rocks, we could see only the darkness, thick and streaked with rain. I strained forward to feel the wet upon my face, to see the glow of the monkey's funeral pyre or glimpse our small skiff, but they were lost, consumed by black night.

The candle we had lighted by the bed flickered in a sudden small gust of wind. I shivered, and Shelley placed his arms about me and I clasped him tight. His body felt so frail, so slim, a sudden fear crossed my heart and, unable to glance into his eyes as he lifted up my chin, I broke away and began speedily to undress. In moments I was beneath the covers watching as Shelley prepared for bed, memorizing each gesture he made. There was a tremendous grace in his movement, swift and sure; his long slender fingers arched and curved so beautifully, they might have been a dancer's legs.

"Do you find Lord Byron fascinating?" he inquired as he removed his shirt.

"Yes," I admitted.

"Could you love him?"

I drew the cover tight about me and stared up at Shelley, who was standing above me studying my reactions, waiting expectantly for my reply. "Would you want me to?" I asked.

"I am only posing a question."

"Not *proposing* an arrangement as you did once with your friend Hogg?"

"It was merely an abstract question and I did not actually propose you have an affair with Hogg. What I did suggest then and possibly do now was that if you felt inclined *towards* an affair you should feel free to have one, and that your doing so would not alter my love for you in any way. I admired Hogg and I admire Lord Byron."

"I would not want to love him," I replied. "Nor would I care to undergo the same anguish I did then."

His gaze fell upon my face and it was I who first turned away. Shortly, he joined me in bed. But the image of Shelley and Byron deep in conversation, as they had been earlier that day, obsessed me, and I found it difficult to dismiss.

"I suppose all England and the Continent—and *you*,

as well, find Lord Byron fascinating," I said. "But there is such a terrible desperation about him."

Shelley remained silent and we lay there watching the flickering candle beside us, not touching, remaining two separate people.

"His voice," I continued, "it awakens such melancholy in me. I seem forced to fight it off. As if his voice were the voice of demons, attacking." I turned away because the brightness of the candle flame had begun to hurt my eyes. "You have heard about his liaison with his sister, Augusta?" I said a few moments later.

"Gossip."

"There was talk of a child."

"If one listens, one can hear the vilest accusations. What does London say about us?"

I turned on my back and stared at the white marble canopy above my head, tracing the black veined lines with my eyes for their beginnings and their ends. It seemed we were once again in the graveyard at St. Pancras and the thought gave me curious comfort, as though my mother might be near. I looked once more into the flickering flame of the candle and felt tears burn in my eyes. "That I am living with another woman's husband," I said softly. "That my Shelley is an atheist— probably in league with incest himself, considering he eloped with two women who are half-sisters."

"You see."

"Umm."

I gently blew the candle out and watched its smoke trail rise above us. "No one understands how impossible it was for you . . . how you suffered . . . how alone we both were before fate brought us together." I had to keep

:[53]:

reminding myself of those facts and Shelley seldom commented for he so completely understood.

Then silence spread about us once again. And darkness, too. And soon my hearing became tuned to all the sounds in the castle; the echoes of all inhabitants past, ghostly whispers and bodyless footsteps. From the moment I had entered the waiting doors of Chillon, I had felt a living, breathing presence. Chillon brooded, Chillon mourned. Chillon quivered in painful memory. Chillon was hostile to intruders and we were unwelcome guests. Chillon would unleash its age-old mysteriousness to discourage us from returning—and if opposed, then— *then* . . . .

I trembled as I thought I heard a low warning sound in the darkness by my pillow. "Shelley . . . " I whispered.

He turned to me. "I love you, sweet Mary," he said softly, his breath now warm upon my cheek.

"I love you, Shelley," I whispered back.

And he drew me closer to him.

4

I had a dream which was not all a dream.
The bright sun was extinguished, and the stars
Did wander darkling in the eternal space,
Rayless, and pathless, and the icy earth
Swung blind and blackening in the moonless air;
Morn came and went—and came, and brought no day,
And men forgot their passions in the dread
of this their desolation . . . .

—BYRON, July, 1816

At this time Albé was morbidly attached to discussions of the end of the world, and he and Shelley would talk of this until the early hours of the morning. All of us would be gathered around the rather formal fireplace in the library at Diodati and the evenings would follow the same pattern of much claret consumed by Albé, followed by excited debate between Albé and Shelley, with Claire and myself silent audience. Polidori, feeling much the outsider in these discussions, would tend to go to his chamber early on.

"Poli is writing the secret life of an opium user," Albé would laugh. But it was no secret that Polidori had great pretensions and even expectations that he would some day publish, and we all suspected he was working on some private manuscript. This evening he had deserted our company earlier than usual and though Albé paid him little heed when he was in his presence, he appeared disturbed that he had defected so early.

"The end will come in too fast time," he said and, glancing at the door that had just seen Polidori's departure, added, "imagine a man like Poli left the last man on the earth!" He turned back to us then. "It will go up in blazes, cities will be consumed, forests extinguished with a crash—*all will be black.*"

Claire shuddered. "I wish you would speak of other things," she said petulantly.

Albé studied her a moment before continuing. "Better yet! Two remaining—Polidori and fair Claire." He confronted her and began to recite what was apparently a recently composed poem of his own, in a voice that was low and intimate and filled with insinuation and secret pleasure. *"And vipers crawled and twined themselves among the multitude, hissing, but stingless—they were slain for food."* He paused and smiled faintly as Claire turned away. *"And war, which for a moment was no more, did glut himself again:—a meal was brought with blood, and each sate sullenly apart gorging himself in*

gloom; no love was left; all earth was but one thought—
and that was death . . . ."

Claire was now sewing very industriously.

"How goes the last stanza, Claire?" he prodded,
coming closer to her, leaning in.

"I only copy what you write, I do not memorize," she
replied, never once glancing up at him, her fingers moving swiftly at her work.

"Most discouraging considering your acting am-
bitions."

"I prefer lighter pieces."

"Unreality? Oblivion? Void?" He turned his back to
her and the fire so that none of us could see his face, and
then his voice rose, vibrant, low, sounding ominous.
"The world was void, the populous and the powerful was
a lump, seasonless, herbless, treeless, manless, lifeless, a
lump of death—a chaos of hard clay."

The night was filled with rain and damp as most of our
nights so far had been, and Shelley, who always had a
problem warming his hands through, sat very close to the
fire so that his fair complexion appeared flushed and his
hair almost yellow-orange in its glow, making him seem
an image of the flame itself.

"That may well be . . . the end may come soon, but
until that time, there is a life and earth and privation,
disease, and crime," Shelley said reflectively. "And an
appalling system exists where one man heaps himself
with luxury at the expense of another."

Albé came back inside the circle of warmth surrounding the fire. "As long as there is work for man,
there is hope," he said.

"Yes, but the poor are set to labour—for what?"

Shelley asked. "Not the food for which they famish, nor the blankets for want of which their children are frozen by the cold, not for those comforts of civilization without which civilized man is far more miserable than the meanest savage. No!" He thought for a moment before continuing. "For the pride of power, for the false pleasures of the hundredth part of society." He stretched towards Albé. "Wealth, your Lordship, is a power usurped by the few, to compel the many to labour for their benefit!"

"And you think if there were no wealth, no power, that men would not fight each other like a pack of hungry dogs warring for a bone? You are a babe in the wood, Shelley! A suckling child!" Albé snapped. "Men would still starve their families to buy guns to promote power—and in defense of their own weakness. I consider myself a poet, a peaceful man, yet I sleep with two pistols by my side each night. It is a ritual. I could not rest without knowing those cold steel barrels are within my reach."

I could not help but interrupt. "Poetry and guns are hardly worthy companions, Milord."

"I am afraid Mary disapproves of guns," Shelley said.

"Oh, and what revolution was ever won without their aid?"

"One day—*Woman's*, Milord."

"Lord preserve me from that spectre! A world governed by women."

Albé sat down then, glancing harshly at me. He was more than irritated at my interruption. He was challenging me openly now to duel with him, and my first instinct, in the pursuit of Shelley's desires, was to back down. I stood up and made to leave the room as Claire's eyes darted like a frightened doe from the men to myself and back again. Albé leaned back in his chair and smiled, looking smugly victorious.

"Not governed, Milord, co-habited in every sense—and with a goodly measure of sensibility," I said sharply.

He straightened, alert, his eyes fastened on my face. "Sensibility has always seemed to me an excuse for all kinds of discontent," he replied.

"If that is so, it seems quite right, for discontent always prefaced achievement, Milord, and content insensibility." I turned once more to leave.

"Extraordinary woman," Albé said as though I had already left the room.

"Yes, she is," Shelley replied.

"But have you noticed, Shelley, how very much like wild fillies, strong-minded women are? They taunt, they bray, they fight like hell, but in the end they do so enjoy being broken."

"Not Mary," Shelley laughed, but still he never looked at me. "Not my Mary."

"One problem with intelligent women—one must be prepared to listen not only to their words, but their thoughts." Albé reached over to the table by his chair and refilled his glass with claret. "I am convinced all women hate words unless their own or words spoken to please their vanities. But song! Heigh Ho! Mary," he shouted. "I shall sing you an Albanian song learned whilst I fought beside the savages."

I came back into the room and stood closer to him. He sat there in the rigid-backed chair until he was sure he had all our attention, then he let out a strange, wild howl, so piercing to the ears that Claire jumped to her feet in terror, dropping her needlework to the floor, and Shelley appeared quite pained. Albé broke into a fit of laughter.

"Shocked?" he finally inquired.

"Disappointed, Milord," I informed him. "We expected an Eastern melody and got the howl of an inebriated wolf!"

If he was angry, he did not have time to show it, for Polidori had reentered the room just then, carrying his black satchel.

"Ah, Poli," Albé greeted him. "What have you there?" Then he laughed. "Poli is the sacred keeper of the nectar of the gods," he told us.

Polidori placed his satchel on the library table and began to unpack it. It contained what I recognized quite easily as an opium pipe and the drug itself. Shelley went over to him to watch the process of the filling of the pipe.

"Coleridge subscribes to its use," Albé said.

"I do not and will not," I insisted.

Albé had come to stand by my side. There was something taunting in his expression. He stood so close that I could feel his breath upon my face.

"Blue is blue," he whispered softly. "As in the sky or fair Claire's eyes, but there are blues in the center of a storm, dear Mary, blues beneath the depth of seas, colder than ice, bluer than death, yet more living than sky and sea. Would you refuse all sight of them, then, for a twinge of a Scotswoman's priggishness?"

"I simply said I did not wish to smoke opium. Certainly that is my right and has little to do with priggishness, Scots, female, or otherwise. You, Milord, will not eat meat. Nor my Shelley either, and I do not censure that or call it by insulting names," I said in a voice clear and loud enough for all to hear. Then I drew away and started for the door. In a moment Shelley was by my side.

"We will start for Chapuis if you wish," he suggested.

"I am fully capable and not in the least fearful of walking there at this hour alone," I replied gently.

"I would prefer you did not," he insisted.

Claire remained, not really comfortable in her decision, but torn by her own needs and her reluctance at leaving Polidori and Albé alone and perhaps in a drugged stupor. She timidly bade Shelley and me adieu and promised to be extremely quiet when she came home so as not to awaken us. I left her, not without concern, and Shelley and I walked through the dense mist towards the lake. It began to rain in torrents just before we reached the cottage and both of us ran the remaining distance and arrived at the door wet to the skin.

In all my tomorrows, I shall remember, when I hear the fall of rain, the sounds of that night . . . of Shelley's running footsteps on the soggy earth as he pulled me on through the rain, the stamping of his feet upon the threshold mat, his laughter as the water ran down his face, his muffled voice as I helped to dry him, the crackle of the fire as we knelt by it to warm our bodies and dry our hair, the splatter of the rain outside our bedroom window as we lay in the darkness, side by side, listening as though we both knew we must memorize that sound.

We were still awake when the rain had ceased and a short time later when the bells at Cologny struck three, and Claire, escorted by Polidori, came home. He departed immediately and she went directly to her room and shut her door tightly and angrily. The bells struck four . . . *five*. Shelley and I were wakeful still—talking in night-whispers when we heard rapid footsteps coming towards our door. Then Claire was there in the doorway, her face distorted most unnaturally by horrible dismay— it beamed with a whiteness that seemed almost like light; her lips and cheeks were of one deadly hue; the skin of her face and forehead was drawn into innumerable wrinkles—the lineaments of terror that could not be contained. Her eyes were wide and staring, drawn almost from their sockets by the convulsions of the muscles, and the eyeballs seemed as if they had been newly inserted, in ghostly sport, in the sockets of a lifeless head. This frightening spectacle endured only a few moments before it was displaced by terror and confusion, violent, indeed, and full of dismay, but *human*.

"Did you touch my pillow?" she asked Shelley in dreadful alarm.

"No, of course not," he told her, sitting up in the dark room beside me, staring at this apparition in the lighted hallway. "You must have had another nightmare, Claire," he assured her.

"No, *no*! The pillow was removed from beneath my head. I was not sleeping. I had merely turned away and when I turned back, my pillow was gone and it seemed removed by—no *human* hand."

She began to tremble and Shelley got up and lighted the fire in our room and the three of us sat before it. Shelley read aloud for a while and then recited one of his poems. Our candles burned low. We feared they would not last until daylight. Just as the dawn was struggling with the moonlight, Claire described again the horror she had felt earlier, and Shelley covered her frightened face for a moment with his hands, speaking to her with the most studied gentleness. But her horror and agony increased, and I finally took her in my arms once again as though she were a small girl. I always struggled to remember that Claire was not as strong as I, that she looked to me for support and that, in truth, it had been I who had encouraged this relationship since we were children.

"He has obtained permission from the Governor of Chillon to visit the castle in the evenings whenever he desires, and he wants to return this coming evening," she whispered in a shaking voice and hid her face against my breast. "Please, Mary, speak to him. He insists we all return to Chillon, and I . . . I have always been afraid of ghosts, and I know, I *swear to you*, the castle is haunted," she cried convulsively and could not be calmed. "I shall not sleep, I cannot," she gasped between sobs.

But at last, too exhausted to remain awake, she did sleep, and after a while, Shelley lifted her from my arms and carried her back to her room and placed her beneath her own covers without waking her.

5

Claire slept late into the afternoon, but I did not, nor could I even rest. Her dream, if indeed it was only a dream, stirred something deep and terrifying in me. The fear of the unknown, a future as awesome as the mountains, the Alps, whose white and shining pyramids and domes towered above all, as if belonging to another earth.

Fulfilling my worst premonitions, a letter arrived for Shelley from Harriet. I wish I could say that Harriet's life formed no portion of the story of Shelley and my lives, but of course, this is an impossibility. Harriet was Shelley's lawful wife, the mother of his children. I had never met her but Shelley spoke of her in their early days of marriage as being fair, bright, innocent and kind-hearted and in many ways childlike. When the time was that she had become this different Harriet, this desperate fugitive from life, we shall never know. But in spite of London's condemnation of us and even in the face of my father's censure, I can confidently state that no act of Shelley's could have been responsible for her rash and sometimes wild behaviour.

He had left her not, as the world wanted to believe, on my behalf, but because she had been unfaithful to him (and that before we met). He had written to her kindly, undertaking to watch over her interests, he had seen she was safe in the protection of her nearest relatives, he had not created a scandal, or taken the children from her, which was much against his own desire. He had been plagued by the bailiffs for her debts and yet given her the small two hundred pound yearly allowance he had exclusive of his father's estate (which was all of his private income) and he always dealt with her emotional outbreaks with kindness and immediacy.

But, then, Harriet had had a history of irrational behaviour. She had asked many mutual acquaintances (who always came to Shelley and myself with the stories), "What do you think of suicide?" and would then reveal an intent to kill herself one day, talking at great length, calmly, resolutely. She had told Shelley that when she had been at school, she had been very unhappy and had contrived sundry attempts at destroying herself. She had told him that she had got up in the night, sometimes with the fixed intention of self-murder. She even talked about this before strangers. Once, at a dinner party, Shelley said, she described her desire for death with such aggravated earnestness, all the while looking so calm, so tranquil, so blooming and so handsome, that the astonished guests smiled!

Shelley shared her letter with me:

DEAR PERCY,

All have turned against me and even my sister has exerted influence to drive me from my father's house, leaving our sweet babes behind. I have taken a small room in Queen Street, Brompton, at no great distance from Hyde Park and the Serpentine River. If you cannot help me I will have no recourse save to seek death speedily so as to finally end all my perplexities and griefs.

I have applied to Sir Timothy for some additional monies but he has turned me down and states that you are quite destitute yourself at this time. But I know that cannot be true. Please contact Sir Timothy and advise him otherwise and commission him to advance me one hundred pounds.

Please do not desert me, Percy.

Your,
HARRIET.

Shelley left for Diodati shortly afterwards and returned before tea in much better spirits. It was not necessary for him to tell me that he had asked Albé for a loan of the money to send Harriet and that Albé had agreed. He sat down and wrote Harriet a letter, even before his clothes were dry from the rain, and gave it to the manservant, who was about to leave for the day, to post on his way home. It was done and it was what Shelley felt he had had to do. I could make no comment, for my mind was too crowded with thoughts that I could not voice without fear that they would then become reality. I knew Albé to be the most generous of men where money was concerned, but I could see the intricate web of dependence he wove about others. Claire and Polidori were his prey, and instinct forbade any consideration of Shelley's also falling victim. Terror of my own entrapment, perhaps, was accountable for my own constant resistance to him. But Shelley admired him intensely and they were together and alone many hours in the day and night, and though I was not jealous of this sharing, I was apprehensive of any influence Albé might exert upon Shelley's thinking or his creativity. It was due to this that I had so many misgivings and could not help but suffer anxiety to know that Shelley was now indebted to him and over a most intimate concern.

My evening was thus darkly shadowed with qualms. I argued against going to Chillon that night but Shelley found my objections groundless (for I could not reveal my true presentiments) and Claire, to my amazement, seemed now convinced not that we should go, but that we *must*.

We set off not much later for Chillon. Due to the rain, we did not take our little boat but travelled by coach, arriving, therefore, at the front gate. Dark melancholy seemed to cloak those gates. The rain was pouring in torrents and a thick mist hid the summits of the mountains and in the distance was the rumbling thunder of a falling avalanche reverberating through the valley and followed by a solemn and vast silence.

Ianthe had been informed of our coming, and though disapproval creased her face, she led us directly to a room called the Duke's Tower, where a fire blazed in the hearth, and placed another log on the fire herself before taking her silent and unbowing leave.

"*Bonne nuit. Ianthe,*" Albé said as she departed.

She kept her silence as she paused at the door. Her eyes were charred coals in spite of the fire reflected in them. She stood there for a moment, then turned and left us with no more than a nod of her head.

"She makes me shiver," Claire complained.

"I find her fascinating," Polidori disagreed.

"You would," Claire sneered. "You are part ghoul yourself."

"Which brings us directly to the point," Albé began.

"That being?" Shelley asked.

"A bit of mental exercise." He sat down before the fire and motioned for us all to join around him. "We will exchange ghost stories," he said when we had formed a circle. "I have just read a German volume which I thought altogether superior. And the thought came to me that this might be a good night—and a good atmosphere—for such an experiment."

Albé leaned back in his chair and smiled. "What we shall do is each of us tell a ghost story. Our own," he said. "We can tell them one at a time here in the evening."

"I find ghost stories . . . most disturbing," Claire said unhappily.

"These will not be of the usual variety. These must be cast with our own ghosts, and the stories brought forth from deep within us," Albé explained.

"It frightens me," Claire pleaded.

Albé sat there studying Claire and I knew he saw, as I did, the fear on her face. "You will begin," Albé told her but gently, almost paternally, "this very night, I think. There will be no pain that way. Pain is most commonly caused by fearful anticipation and little else."

He stood up and gathered the candles and handed one to each of us which he then lighted. "We are agreed then? We shall pursue our harmless game?"

"I think not," I said instantly as I noted the candle shaking in Claire's hand.

"A bit of adventure is all!" Albé added, then he crossed to the door and smiled. "Follow me," he commanded and left the room before us, starting down the darkened, shadow-swept corridor, holding his candle high.

The rest of us followed single file through the darkness, the cryptlike passageways black in a moonless, starless night, our candles in the wind that crossed our paths creating distortions of moving light on all sides of us, leaving a stirred and restless dark behind. We were rowers on a black sea, where we seemed to have awakened the monsters of the deep.

Yet I for one, knew something held me fast, that I must not desert or draw back or away. We were being led into a chapter of our future that must be lived before we would be able to pass on. What lay ahead in the undiscovered, the yet to be reached and experienced, was a penalty that must be forfeited. Perhaps for our youth, perhaps for all youth that must die as ours was certain to.

Shelley walked before me, his step fast and even, never wavering, following Albé resolutely. It was, I realized then, quite amazing how Albé had trained the rest of his body to compensate for the malformation of his one clubfoot. The foot seemed to pull along the hard stone floor. He was, in fact, difficult to keep pace with, and all of us had to walk with almost running steps to remain close behind.

We entered the courtyard and walked for a few uncovered steps. Albé was leading us to the dungeons. I cupped my hands about the flame of the candle to keep it from extinguishing. The dark was as impenetrable outside as it had been in the maze of blackness we had just passed through.

The doors to the dungeons had been left open as they had that first night. We slowed down as we reached the stairs and, as they were pitted and uneven, some far narrower than others, descended with caution.

We were surrounded by darkness and by silence. The rain though persistent was slow and could not be heard beyond the massive depth of window. I listened hard for the sound of the swelling waters but they were muted and without breath. The wind had stilled. Our candle flames burned evenly and no grey smoke trails streaked the outer dark.

Albé stopped before the Prisoner of Chillon's Pillar (I could, in fact, hear him counting the pillars as we passed). "Here," he said, and we gathered around him.

It must have been damp and chill. All logic tells me so, but I felt feverish and as though in an overheated room. Yet the heat was an interior and living thing. Shelley took my hand and in the dim light his smile seemed detached and disconnected. I moved closer to him. His face was flushed red and the palm of his hand damp with perspiration.

Albé had us all place our candles in a ring on the stone floor and then sit down behind them. He insisted Claire sit with her back to the Prisoner's Pillar and that she be the one to begin.

"Relax," Albé whispered to her. "Relax, Claire." His voice was hypnotic and his eyes burning.

Tears filled Claire's eyes and though she opened her mouth to speak, the words would not come.

Albé smiled at her with a tenderness he seldom displayed. "It would pleasure me much, Claire," he said gently.

Shelley, who sat next to her, clasped her hand tightly in his own.

"You can stop whenever you wish," I assured her. "And if you desire to leave, I shall not hesitate to leave with you."

She trembled still, but there was colour in her face once again.

Polidori then took out a pipe and laboriously filled it with the opium and handed it to her. She glanced nervously across our closed circle to me.

"It must be your own decision, Claire," I told her.

For a long time she sat there indecisively looking from Albé to myself. Finally, she took the pipe and drew slowly upon it.

There is no way for me to recall exactly how long we sat there before Claire began to speak. I had refused the drug and so time may have seemed that much longer to me. At first I strained to hear the sounds I had not first been able to hear—the rain, the water, the wind, even the night creatures who surely lived in the dark and stony walls around us. But soon I was conscious of an opposite effect taking place. I could hear my own pulse and it grew louder and louder and filled my ears with its thunderous drum roll.

I was frightened and I knew why.

This dungeon was to represent the secret cell within ourselves where all our private haunting took place.

6

"Begin, Claire," Albé ordered in a gentle but commanding voice.

Claire seemed transfixed by the candle's flame.

"Give her a moment." I reached across the circle and touched Claire's hand.

She raised her eyes slowly and her glance caught mine and for a moment they were both entangled. Then she looked away and into the upper darkness. "Once upon a time," she began.

"Good Lord!" Polidori spat.

"Once upon a time there was a beautiful and innocent young girl," she continued and then suddenly stopped.

"Go on, Claire," Albé urged.

"One day she chanced to take a walk in the forest near a castle where a grand young nobleman lived. She had seen him once in the village astride a golden horse, dressed in golden armour, his golden hair glistening in the sun. She had fallen quite desperately in love at first sight. Of course, this was a hopeless situation, for the nobleman was far above her station."

Claire now closed her eyes and her voice took on a sureness it had never had and I found myself listening, enraptured, able to see before my closed lids all the images her velvet voice evoked.

"On this day," she was saying, "the sun was very high and as the maiden left the forest, she was so bedazzled by the brilliance of the golden turrets of the castle burning in the brightness of the sun, that at first she thought she heard someone calling her name distantly and from the heart of the forest. And so she turned and started back along the same path.

"But the forest suddenly grew dark and threatening. The young girl whirled about, thinking she might return to the path of the castle after all, but giant gnarled branches barred her way and so she went slowly forward and for one fleeting instant, a pair of eyes beckoned to her from the darkness. She quickly turned away and searched in another direction. But there were those same eyes again, amid heavy foliage, and this time *they seemed to plead*.

"The maiden was terrified, more from the intensity of the plea in those eyes than of the terror about her, and she turned away, and with her head down so as to see nothing but the path, she began to run. She was bewildered and frightened, and finally—*lost*. The gnarled arms of the trees reached out for her and tore her clothes, small jagged twigs seized and snarled her hair.

feet and began to sob. Shelley was closer to her and so reached her before I could.

"It was only a game, Claire," he soothed.

But she could not control her sobs and so Shelley helped her outside, away from the dungeon and into the night air. I was, therefore, left for a moment alone with Albé and Polidori.

"Milord," I said to Albé, "you are unduly hard. You knew from the start this would be too difficult for Claire."

"Women never see consequences," he replied sharply, "never look at things straightforward or as they ought."

"She is a woman in love, Milord."

"Woman is naturally a creature of love. They *die* of love, and they love, *Mistress Mary*, for themselves, though they may offer any number of other irrelevant reasons."

A hard look passed between us. Albé turned to leave the dungeon but stumbled on a loose stone. I reached my hand out to help him but he drew away and steadied himself, and so I stood back and watched him walking slowly and painfully away.

7

Like one who, on a lonely road,
Doth walk in fear and dread
And having once turned round, walks on,
And turns no more his head;
Because he knows a frightful fiend
Doth close behind him tread.
—COLERIDGE, *The Ancient Mariner*

I reread the verse in Coleridge's *Ancient Mariner*, now bringing my own interpretation to it. Albé had told us one night of visiting Coleridge in his country home in England and how Coleridge had recommended the use of drugs to heighten one's creative powers.

Like one who, on a lonely road,
Doth walk in fear and dread . . .

:[81]:

The lines stuck in my mind like fragments of a haunting melody.

All day I had been agitated. I could not endure to think of the occurrence of the previous night, and yet it was quite impossible to forget. I kept as much to myself as I could, not wanting to discuss the events with Shelley or even Claire.

Coleridge had feared the past, but what I trembled at were the secrets withheld by the future. A shivering would come over me whenever I paused to open a door, as though I might find a spectre waiting for me on the other side. I stepped fearfully into rooms and strained my eyes looking into shadows.

The afternoon had set in wet and misty and Claire had gone up to Diodati leaving Shelley and me to ourselves. I stood by the library window unseen by Claire as she left but watching her as she crossed the garden to the vineyard dividing the two houses. She seemed to steal out into the dying day. No "good-byes" had been called and, had I not been standing there, I would not have heard or seen her departure. There was a distraction in her step that could not be dismissed. She wore black about her pale, white face and she darted over the damp, over-grown grass, carelessly allowing her skirts to drag so that a rim of dark wetness encircled her feet. She looked like some poor, blinded moth, attracted by the light. I thought to call her back and serve her tea, or of accompanying her to Diodati myself, but Shelley spoke at that moment, having entered the room without my hearing him. And when I turned back to the window

Claire had disappeared in the veil of falling rain behind the farthest patch of trees at the rear of the garden.

A chill wind passed through the room and I drew my shawl tightly about me.

"What is it, Mary?" Shelley asked.

"I am not sure. I am frightened though. I think we are conjuring up our own ghosts."

"Albé meant it for a game."

"No child's game, though, no mere entertainment." I walked away and to the fire. The light in the room was grey even though the flames burned bright. "All day I have had terrible forebodings." I shivered and he came and stood before me, his eyes fastened on my face, his glance shutting out the rest of the world for me.

"What we are doing is dangerous, Shelley, dangerous!"

"Good Lord, why?"

"Because we are playing a frightening game of little gods, creating new images, exploring the unexplored."

"And why not?"

"Are any of us prepared for the outcome? Claire? I watched her closely last night. She could easily become unhinged. And just now, she was flushed before she went out in the chill. She is in a perpetual state of fever."

"She was before."

"She has always been a delicate girl—I will admit that. But this is something else, something quite different."

I walked away and over to the window and latched it, as though I considered the twilight capable of listening and the wind, even gentled as it was by the rain, a carrier of words.

"She exposed her deepest emotions last night," I said.

"And is that bad? What is there in this world that any of us at our age should feel shame to expose? And who sets the standards, the morals? It is a crime to commit incest with your sister or brother, and yet what could be more natural than the love that must grow between brother and sister, reared closely, sharing the most intimate of each other's lives?"

"We are not discussing Albé. We are discussing Claire." I spoke sharply.

"She told Albé, within the framework of her story," he said, "the depth of her love, her fear of abandonment, her insecurity in the face of his brilliance—perhaps she could not have told him otherwise."

"She threatened suicide," I said.

Shelley remained unruffled. "I did not interpret the story that way. She gave me to believe that she considered she would die of love if Albé deserted her. But if that ever were to occur, I assure you such would not be the case."

Shelley sat down by the fire and I sat at his feet, holding my knees to me as though needing to keep myself bound together, and stared into the fire.

"There are so many things buried deep inside all of us," I began. "Somewhere in the midnight of our hearts are stirrings that must remain in eternal darkness. Elsewhere, there are things that should be brought to life. But how does anyone know which is deserving of life? It *was* a death wish, and Claire might never have known she harboured such feelings had she not been forced to drag them from her inner darkness and expose them to a world of light."

"But what other way to test the true measure of a person?" Shelley asked quietly.

"Must there be a measure?"

He coughed then and his leg, which I was leaning against, trembled. The previous year an eminent physician had pronounced that Shelley was dying rapidly of a consumption and that abcesses were formed on his lungs. He had in the past suffered acute spasms. But a complete change had taken place shortly after we met, and every symptom of pulmonary disease vanished. Still, when he coughed this way, I always grew disturbed.

"It is the rain," I said, "this insistent, unyielding rain." I rose angrily, happy really to have an enemy at whom I could direct my rage. "Perhaps you were right and Italy would be better. There must be sun there. There has to be sun somewhere."

Shelley laughed until the tears came into his eyes. "*Blithe spirit, child of love and light, how much I love thee,*" he said at last. "Love, after all, is the only fit, the sole law which should govern the moral world."

The room had warmed and we were both caught up in its glow.

Shelley spoke and I listened, captured by his words as always, by the depth of his feelings, the keenness of his mind and the temper of his indignation. I have known no other man who loved all mankind so devotedly, who was so impatient of all oppression or who so desperately tried to unveil religious frauds, slavery and degradation.

:[85]:

The fire burned low and day passed into evening. I stood at the window as Shelley lighted the lamps. The mist, the rain had ceased, and a bloated moon lighted the night. But the sky was cloudless and the night the dark grey of a mourner's veil, and in the blacked-out harbour I could see our small boat. It seemed to have a phantom gibbet for a mast and a shroud for its brave sail.

8

The next day, the sun rose blood-red above the glistening white peaks of the mountains. It was to be a summer's day, the first we had had since our arrival in Switzerland, I suggested to Claire that the two of us go off on our own as it seemed on such a day as this, warm breezes and clear sky, that all shadow could be dispelled. I proposed we take the coach to Chillon to see it in bright daylight, so that when we did return again at night, the dark interiors would not seem so filled with shapeless terrors.

The guard at the gate let us enter. A child, otherwise unattended, played in the dirt at his feet and a small mongrel dog lay sleeping against the shade of the high wall. There was a guide, the guard informed us, if we cared to wait, who was now showing another group through the castle. He thought us travellers and, indeed, at that moment we felt quite properly cast. But we declined the wait and crossed the familiar cobblestoned courtyard alone.

We were two young girls on a summer day's outing. The sunlight blurred our vision and for no reason at all we laughed and hurried across the sun-splashed stones to the castle door.

It was unlatched and so we entered.

The stone passageways were flooded with sunlight that came in great arcs from the high carved windows. Claire and I still shared laughter. We reflected the brightness. Claire wore a butter-yellow dress of a gossamer fabric and her blond hair glistened in golden ringlets about her head as she glided before me.

We had never fully explored the castle and so knew little more about what it held than the chambers we had slept in that very first night, the Duke's Tower, the passages leading to the dungeons and those vaulted caves themselves. We now investigated that part of the castle around the courtyard between the dungeons and the Duke's Tower. These held immense rooms filled with windows overlooking the lake, rooms that were once the scene of glittering ceremonies and assemblies and balls. For feasts there were banquet halls of vast dimensions and luminosity. Each room had a distinguishing mark of beauty. In one, a richly ornamented ceiling was supported by three slender columns of black marble from Saint Triphon, in another, a colossal fireplace and graceful double lancet-arched Gothic windows. Benches transformed its window recesses into small loggias, and overall was a handsome mural decoration composed of squares on beams laid out in oblique strips, alternatively grey and white or pink and white. Over these murals were hung richly ornamented tapestries on blue and scarlet satin.

We ventured into every hidden corner, opened wide each carved or humble door. We were dispelling our own shadows, for people can be haunted too and need the day and the sun and the truth to sweep away the dust of fear and silence the echo of spirit cries.

In each room there was the Spartan hand of Ianthe. Things were as they should be if Chillon's stone corridors should suddenly come alive once again with the rustle of satin and brocade and the click of polished boots and ladies' pointed shoes. We did not encounter her, however, or a single visitor, though once we heard voices in the distance, muffled yet spirited and clearly belonging to the living. Our own voices were sounding lighter, gayer, summer swallows in small abandon before winter comes.

Finally we reached a covered staircase leading down to a set of heavy doors sealed ominously shut. We silently agreed to try them, though, and Claire descended the narrow stone stairs first. At the base and facing the doors, she breathed deeply. She was exhilarated and flushed with excitement.

"Pray, dear sister, follow me," she exclaimed and then after turning the handle with all her strength it gave and, with a cry of triumph, she flung the doors open. She stood there transfixed, and me right beside her, our laughter left behind us like footsteps on a snow-covered path.

We stood on the threshold of the most beautiful small chapel I had ever seen. The sun flooded its Gothic interior through a deeply arched window above a small white altar. The ceiling was vaulted, the walls frescoed, and all the pillars carved. I looked about in wonder. Serenity dwelt here and sanctuary for the most troubled heart.

Claire stepped cautiously inside and I followed. We walked softly across the smooth polished stone floors and in the pathway of the window light. We passed an unusual pillar that had carved on it three heads fused so that their features could not be separated from one another, and then stood side by side, before the altar. There was a square of sunlight, like a prayer rug at our feet.

"Mary . . . "

"Yes?"

"I know how you and Shelley feel—about a legal marriage, that is. I mean, I know you do not think the church or the law can bind two people, or rather *should* bind two people . . . that it has to be . . . well . . . . " She paused nervously and took a small breath. "There is something to be said about a legal marriage, true? Especially, most *particularly* . . . . "

"Where a child is imminent."

Claire sighed with relief. "You have guessed."

"Shelley and I both did. As far back as England."

She cast her eyes down and clasped her hands. "I manoeuvred the meeting between Albé and Shelley," she began, as though in confession. "You guessed that as well. But my motives were not entirely selfish." She looked up at me. "All I ever truly wanted was to please Albé. I was so sure bringing him together with Shelley would do just that."

"A man must love you for yourself, Claire. Less is humbling," I told her.

She lowered herself to the stone floor and sat there, the golden yellow of her skirt billowing like an aureole of sunlight about her. I sat down cautiously and somewhat stiffly beside her, conscious that we faced an altar, conscious of all the atheistic anti-religious viewpoints voiced by Shelley and of my own consent to those beliefs. And yet, something deep and hallowed and tremendously private was happening to me in this room.

I doubted not religion, not Christ, but my own repudiation of them both.

We sat there quietly, neither speaking for a time.

"I am not sure Annabelle will ever divorce Albé," she said at last. "And I am quite sure he will always love Augusta. But you see Albé has so *very* much love to give that even a corner of his heart would warm me sufficiently."

"Claire—"

"No, do let me continue. You really do not know Albé. I suppose no one ever will know Albé, but I do understand a great deal about him, and loving him as I do, can transpose false appearances to real feelings." She smoothed out her skirt and then folded her hands neatly on her lap. She did not look at me. Her eyes were on the ray of sun and the brightness caused her to squint. She considered a passing thought and then discarded it, closed her eyes, and continued—suddenly seeming much older.

"He was born, as I am sure you have heard, with a clubfoot and his mother went to great means to correct this deformity—but only succeeded in making it worse."

She opened her shining violet eyes and turned away from the beam of light and towards me. There were tears misting her glance. "Having done so," she said in a lowered voice, "it seemed she then could love him no longer and passed him over to the care of a governess when he was nine. Her name was May Gray and she was mad. She hated Albé and was cruel to him during the day, ridiculing his lameness, striking him with hurting words and glancing blows and then at night when they were alone, she would crawl into his bed and manipulate his body in various sexual experiments. Being a boy, the excitement seemed like an adventure to him and he allowed her to continue."

"How outrageous!"

"It is incredible, but this went on for two years, this terrorizing of him during the day interspersed with lectures from the Bible, for she was a staunch and dedicated church-goer, and these . . . lecheries at night. You can see how he would come to dissociate love and sex and how deeply he would crave true love, how desperately a woman would have to prove she truly loved him, how far she would have to go—for him to believe in her." She wiped away a tear with the back of her hand and tossed her head so that for a moment each blond curl came alive.

"That is how I explain Augusta," she said, drawing in her breath quickly and then slowly letting it escape, "though not to Albé. Augusta is one subject I am not permitted to discuss. But he tells me a great deal about his life. All the terrible things, too. As though he wants me to love him in the face of all these unnatural and sometimes disgusting obstacles. And that is just the point, you see?" Claire breathed deeply. "I do."

"Has he said he would recognize the child?" I asked quietly and after a moment's pause.

"No."

"But he knows?"

"Oh, yes. Of course."

"Before you came to Switzerland?"

"No—since—the first night here."

"Have you discussed the future?"

She shook her head. "There is so much," she sighed, "to exorcise first about the past."

She looked at me directly then, clear-eyed. "I am convinced he will never return to England and I am certain Augusta will never join him on the Continent." Her hand reached out for mine. "You and Shelley will not return to London"—she softened then, her eyes pleading— "promise?"

"I cannot promise you that, or speak for Shelley."

Her face clouded. "I could never face Father," she said in a small voice.

I covered her hand with my own, as if a pledge. "You will never have to do that alone," I said with deep emotion.

There was an understanding that passed between us then that we had never had before. She fought back the tears of gratitude that showed in her eyes. I rose and helped her to her feet and as we dusted ourselves and straightened out our skirts, I noted a gust of wind on the small of my back and turned. The inner wall of the chapel, the wall that had been behind me, and which I now faced, was draped in white cloth halfway down to the floor, and there the curtain blew as though wind came from behind it. I went over and drew back the drape. A doorway stood partially opened, no more than half the height of either Claire or myself. The opening was narrow and the area beyond the doorway pitchy blackness. Claire was directly behind me as I leaned forward for a better view.

"What is it, Mary?"

At first all I could see was blackness, a deep cavernous dark—then my eyes became accustomed to the lack of light.

"Oh, I see now," I called over my shoulder. "It is a small room—low ceilinged." I pressed forward. "It appears to be a cell."

Claire drew back, but my curiosity had been aroused. I pushed the door open as far as it would go, then got down on my hands and knees and proceeded to crawl into the hidden room. Claire, obviously more fearful of being left alone, was close behind me. Once inside, we could straighten, but the ceiling was heavily beamed and only inches from our heads.

My eyes had finally grown used to the dark. Directly across the room, an area of no more than four metres, was another door, slightly ajar so that light seeped in. I started across the room, and having not glanced down at the floor, had not seen the pit that lay between both doors, and almost stumbled. Fortunately Claire had grabbed my skirt and pulled me back.

At that moment the door I had meant to reach opened and Ianthe stood in the doorway.

"Visitors are forbidden here," she said.

I ignored her hostility as best I could. "Where does that door lead?" I inquired.

"To the gallows," she announced and settled heavily back on the heels of her strong black shoes. "That," she explained, pointing to the pit between us, "is a pit where prisoners were once lowered, then sealed inside."

Very carefully, I skirted the pit, holding Claire's hand tightly and pressing against the outside wall until I was in the safe area, facing Ianthe. "If you will open the door wide, we will pass through," I said. But she remained staring at us enigmatically and barring our passage from the cell.

"I do not intend," I continued calmly, "for my sister and myself to crawl from this room the way we came, Ianthe, so open the door."

It was a long moment before she actually did so. Claire scurried past her and into the long, narrow room beyond. I took my time and with an imperious air followed.

We were in the gallows and would have to pass through the dungeons to come out again into the courtyard. The scaffold was behind us and Claire and I tried very hard not to glance back over our shoulders.

"Thank you," I conceded to Ianthe.

She stood there looking at us with tortured memories reflected in her eyes. I thought it might be best to speak a few words with her before leaving, although Claire was already edging nervously towards the exit.

"I am sorry we could not have had you show us about, for I am certain you know more about Chillon than the guide," I ventured conversationally.

"There are many things I know better than most."

"I am quite sure of that."

"I need no books or poets," she turned her head now as if listening to far-off voices, voices apparently trapped in the cell we had just departed. "Doors breathe and the wind speaks and the past whispers in my ears." She sealed the door and came closer to me.

"Once, when the moon was young and I with it, there was a Lord of Chillon who had right to such title. Since, these walls have been under my sole protection. Your Lord Byron is an evil influence and should be forbidden to enter Chillon's gates. I have told the Governor so."

"The Governor appears not to agree."

"The world is filled with as many fools as it is with evil-doers," she said. She apparently did not intend to follow us out. I turned and stepped to Claire's side, conscious of Ianthe's raven's eyes upon our backs.

We had been so blinded by the smoke of terror that the cell and Ianthe's sudden appearance had created, that we entered the dungeons gladly and without fear.

The sun had begun to fade and one last ray appeared to seep from a crevice of a far window and creep over the damp rock floor. The room was deep and took forever, it seemed, to cross. But once safely at the base of the stairs leading up to the sunlit courtyard, we paused to look back. The dungeons were bathed in a green-blue light cast from the sea and the sky and the steeply arched passageways were stately and grand, the pillars dignified and supremely beautiful.

There was contained in that area where men had once been chained, spending hours with rats at their feet and the sound of water rising in their ears, a beauty, hallowed and all-enveloping and not at all unlike the aura that we had felt in the little chapel.

I was not alone in these feelings, as Claire stood by my side unable to leave as I was, and when we finally did ascend the stairs, cross the courtyard, and depart Chillon, we had the strange feeling that we had both just left behind a solemn shrine.

9

I was unprepared for the jolt to my senses that being alone in the presence of Lord Byron created. Shelley had accompanied Claire into Vevey on an errand and was gone a good part of the day. I had thought to busy myself at my desk with answering a long list of neglected correspondence and had only sat down to the task when there *he* was standing facing me, his back to the fire, as the servant closed the library doors and left the two of us alone.

"This meeting has been long overdue," he said.

"I thought it would be the least likely meeting you would encourage," I replied. I realized I still sat at my desk, which was an act of rudeness, yet I could not bring myself to rise.

"Which proves you are a woman after all, for only

omen rush to such conclusions." He smiled, his dark, deep-set eyes riveted on mine.

"Was there a doubt in your mind that I be truly woman?"

"Never. But the world and a cold-hearted Mary might need proof."

"A cold heart? No, your Lordship, my heart is very full. But it is a distant land where few may enter to warm themselves."

"Can you for some small moments not think of Shelley?" His smile grew softer but only lighted half his face, his eyes remaining dark as midnight. "I am a rather singular man whose pride demands a woman's sole and rapt attention," he added.

His words jarred me strongly and his peculiar deep-throated voice unsettled me.

"Shall I offer you tea, consolation, some compliments I have been remiss in giving? You see, I am at a loss in knowing what you wish of me."

He walked slowly across the room and towards me. I was painfully conscious of his lameness, in those short moments it took for him to reach the desk I sat at, and a confusing tenderness tapped uninvited at my heart.

"Have you ever been drunk, Mary?" he asked.

"No, never."

"You need to be a little tipsy, you know, otherwise how will you quicken the flow of blood? A bit more wine, Mary, and fewer tears."

"Few have seen my tears, your Lordship. And those few, I am certain, did not bandy words of them about."

He was leaning over me, one hand resting on the desk, as the other brushed a straying lock of hair back from my forehead. "I wonder, Mary, if you could once but shed a few for me," he said.

At that moment I wished to stand and move away from his touch and his voice and the musky odour of his cologne more than any other wish I might ever have, but his presence bending over me, his hand now on my shoulder, barred this possibility. "Please, your Lordship," I whispered haltingly, "allow me to rise."

He stood away without a moment's hesitation and I rose and crossed the room and warmed my hands at the fire.

"Why do you call me your Lordship now and Albé in mixed company?" he asked, his voice puzzled and low.

"A certain formality must be preserved."

"Here and now, I take it you mean?"

"Yes, your Lordship! Here and now." I turned from the fire to find him only a short distance away.

"Shelley might desire otherwise," he said.

"Perhaps, but if I am any mistress at all, it is of my own desires."

For the longest moment our eyes met. It was Lord Byron who finally shifted his and then sat down on a chair close by. He leaned back with much possessiveness as though, indeed, the chair, the room, was his, and stretched his legs out and clasped the arms so tightly that I could see the whiteness of his knuckles.

"If feelings are not your pleasure dome—your Kubla Khan—then what is, Mary?" he asked with no tone of mockery. Truth, there was a warmth, an honest interest that took me by surprise.

I smiled, but when I spoke I perceived a tremor in my voice that served me notice that though I might be mistress of my own desires, I was not mistress of my emotions!

"I would not say my feelings do not dwell in pleasure, but I would suppose it is my imagination where I can live in greatest harmony."

"You hope to be an author, or a poet, then?"

"I dare not be so presumptuous—but yes, I shall write." And then, as though the thought had only that moment been conceived, "Some day soon," I added. And then, "Shall I ring for tea?"

"I would prefer something a bit stronger."

I went over to the liquor cabinet. "Claret, then? or brandy?"

"Or love."

I turned quickly. "Please, your Lordship, you do me great disservice." My hand and voice trembled as I spoke.

"You are so young, Mary. Nineteen only. And a very extraordinary girl. I find you make a faulty barometre of my emotions."

"I am sorry," I said quietly and with meaning.

"Why on earth should you be? Unloose your emotions, Mary. Unleash them, and you will make Shelley a happier man and yourself a free woman."

"But I am that already," I declared.

His eyes grew clouded. "If you believe that to be the truth, the battle has already been lost."

"Were we speaking of wars, your Lordship?"

"We were—and *are*, for hawks will not quit their prey. And so they must fight it out until the lone survivor becomes the victor."

"But, in such a case, loses the victory? Right, your Lordship?"

"Wrong, Mary."

I turned aside and lifted a decanter. "Would brandy do? I see the claret bottle is empty." He did not reply and when I faced him again, he was standing by the door.

"We will go to Chillon tonight," he said.

"Do you think that a good idea?" I asked skeptically.

"It is what I want to do," was his frank reply and then he departed.

10

Dearest Augusta

*. . . I can bear fatigue and welcome privation, and
have seen some of the noblest views in the world.
But in all this--the recollection of bitterness and
more especially of recent and more home desolation,
which must accompany me through life, have
preyed upon me here; and neither the music of the
Shepherd, the crashing of the avalanche, nor the
torrent, the mountain, the glacier, the forest, nor the
cloud, have for one moment lightened the weight
upon my heart, nor enabled me to lose my own
wretched identity in the majesty, the power, and the
glory, around, above, and beneath me.*

*Excerpt, Journal kept for Augusta
by Byron, Summer, 1816*

Albé was in the habit of rising each day at about two in the afternoon and seldom went to bed before three in the morning. Claire would, therefore, go up to the villa each day and while he worked, copy his pages from the previous day. He was well into the Third Canto of *Childe Harold* and the view from Diodati inspired him to write at quite an amazing pace. Amusingly, he would give Shelley dated copies of this work to show him how prolifically creative he was. Shelley and I would join them in the late afternoon, at which time it was tacitly understood that Claire and I would remain observers while the men talked. Both Claire and I equally enjoyed listening to our men, so these conversations were agreeable to us. But to Polidori, who seldom had a contribution to make, they were unendurable.

One could not help but note a chilling hostility building in the man and observe, as well, that this hostility was having its effect on Albé, which in turn affected us all. Albé seemed roused to a higher mood and temper and his work, which he read aloud to us in these afternoons, reflected it. In place of shadowy griefs and vague ennui had come an actual warfare with the world. He seemed half mad at times and would rant about being torn between metaphysics, mountains, love unextinguishable (*Augusta*), thoughts unutterable (*!*) and the nightmares of his own delinquencies (*?*). Shelley, with all his spiritualizing power, argued daily to neutralize his turmoil of conflicting passions.

Polidori appeared to enjoy Albé's great digressions and agonies, but was indescribably venomous in his hatred of Shelley for "meddling." He was at most times, though, so ludicrous in his behaviour that the men did not take him quite so seriously as Claire and I did. All of us knew Polidori had pretensions to being a great tragic poet. At times he would insist we listen to his verse. I disliked the man more than ever now and felt his evil was a living thing that walked among us.

One late afternoon I shall never forget. Shelley and Albé were intense in a discussion of Sheridan, whom Albé admired greatly and whom we had just heard had died, and Polidori sat sulking by an open window, glancing out at the fits of wilfulness the day inspired, thunder showers and baffling breezes now changed into a warm southern gust, summer clouds, the sky a deep chasm of blue and the lake a gentle reflection.

"Sheridan once told me," Albé was saying, "that on the night of the grand success of *School for Scandal*, he was knocked down and put into the watchhouse for making a row in the street and being found intoxicated. Now, *there* was a man who could drink! I will miss him. He was probably one of the only pleasures I shall miss in England. He hated poetry, you know. Mine included! But he was sure I should make an orator. He never ceased harping on it."

"Well, you would at that," Shelley confirmed.

"Perhaps, perhaps. I remember my old tutor, Dr. Drury, had the same notion when I was a boy. I did speak once or twice, as all young peers do as a kind of introduction into public life, and the reception was not too discouraging. I sometimes wonder to myself if I should have gone on with it."

"Sheridan was an idiot," Polidori interrupted. "Surely nothing can be as important as your poetry."

"Unless it is yours, eh Poli?"

"I have faith in myself, if that is what you mean. And I wager time will prove me right."

"I will make you a wager, Poli, a very small one—the worth of your poetry," Albé laughed.

Polidori rose to his feet, his eyes full of pain. "After all, you write successful poetry," he said, adding stiffly, "What is there you can do that I cannot?"

"Three things," Albé replied immediately. "I can swim across that lake; I can snuff out that candle with a pistol shot at the distance of twenty paces; and I can give you a damned good thrashing!"

Shelley laughed and Polidori turned on him, his eyes flashing, "Damn you, Shelley, damn you! I should challenge you, that is what I have a mind to do. You and your arrogant laughter and your damned gentlemanly presence."

"Recollect," Albé interrupted harshly, speaking before Shelley had time to reply, "that though Shelley has some scruples about dueling, *I* have none and shall be at all times ready to take his place."

Polidori stood as though riveted to the floor. It was the first time that Albé had taken Shelley's side against him. Then, he turned and left the room with a heavy step, slamming the door violently.

"Well, he is back to his pestle and poisons," Albé commented. "You know that is part of what he does with his privacy? He studies various and sundry methods that make death easy."

"You are too hard on him, Albé." Shelley shook his head.

"One needs to be. Men like Polidori live for such treatment and would die for want of it," Albé replied.

There was an awkward silence. None of us felt in the least bit comfortable. Albé looked around at us and then went on, hoping, I assumed, to entertain, to lift the tension.

"Polidori extending a challenge!" he laughed coarsely. "I have been called in as second at least twenty times in violent quarrels and have always contrived to settle the business without compromising the honour of the parties or leading them to mortal consequences. But I am not at all sure how I would have handled the matter of Polidori!" He crossed to the liquor cabinet and poured himself a claret.

"I have had to carry challenges from gentlemen to noblemen, from captains to captains, from lawyers to counsellors, and once from a clergyman to an officer in the Lifeguards. It may seem strange, but I found the latter by far the most difficult." He emptied his glass and poured another.

"It was all due to a woman named Susan, a more cold-blooded, heartless whore there never was! I asked her to say two words, that was all that was required to save the life of the priest and the Lifeguard. She refused and nothing would move her. But I managed to quiet the combatants and have them mutually agree to withdraw their challenges, much to her great disappointment. She was the damnedest bitch that I ever saw and I have seen a great many!"

He drank down the claret and breathed deeply. He had enjoyed being on stage, and now he glanced around for approval. Some of the tension had, in fact, lifted.

"There, that is better," he exclaimed and came back and sat down opposite Shelley.

There was a heavy silence in the room. Albé had withdrawn momentarily into the shadow past of memory. His face was set sadly and his eyes darkly unhappy.

"Mary received a letter this morning from her sister Fanny," Shelley mentioned as an effort to distract.

Albé glanced over at me, studying me closely, and for the moment I thought he might not have heard Shelley speak. Then he smiled rather brightly, his face immediately coming alive, seeming vital once again.

"Oh—Oh!" he exclaimed. "There are more at home like you two ladies! The male population stands little chance I see."

"Fanny is older than I. She was a love child of my mother's. We do not share the same father."

"Shall I take that literally?" Albé grinned.

"As literally as I take your words, I would say."

"Ah—*good stroke*. And the letter?"

"It contained news of Coleridge," Shelley proffered.

Albé was instantly attentive. "I hope you brought it with you," he said. He had softened and he sat almost like an obedient child waiting for permission to be granted. I took Fanny's letter from my pocket and read part of it aloud:

> . . . I am sending you a copy of Mr. Coleridge's *Christabel*. Lamb says it ought never to have been published; that no one understands it. Coleridge is living at Highgate. He is living with an apothecary, to whom he pays five pounds a week for board, lodging and medical advice. The apothecary is to take care that he does not take either opium or

spiritous liquors. Coleridge, however, was tempted, and wrote to a chemist he knew in London, to send him a bottle of laudanum to Mr. Murray's in Albemarle Street, to be inclosed in a parcel of books to him; his landlord, however, felt the parcel outside and discovered the fatal bottle. Mr. Morgan told me the other day that Coleridge improved in health under the care of this apothecary and was writing fast a continuation of *Christabel* . . . .

I refolded the letter carefully and slipped it back into my pocket.

All of us sat quietly for a time, Coleridge's image graven upon our minds.

"It pains me to think of him thus," Albé finally said, "but his addiction does not mean to infer that if we continue experimenting with the same drugs he uses, we shall become addicted. *Christabel*, which I have read in manuscript, and *The Ancient Mariner* could not have been conceived otherwise, and for Coleridge drugs are his world. For myself, and since I have an unsuppressable passion for excitement, they only sharpen the edges of my experience."

"At whose expense?" I asked quietly.

"My own," he replied.

I looked at Shelley and then turned away.

"Grimm, you know, says that for a man to be a genius, he must have a violent and tormented spirit. That is true of Coleridge, by God!" Albé was saying to Shelley. "And if it holds for Coleridge, then I should be a poet *per eccellenza*, for I have always had a spirit which not only tormented itself, but everybody else in contact with it, a violent spirit which has in fact left me almost without any spirit at all," he laughed.

He poured himself another glass of claret and began to pace back and forth across the room. Lines of pain creased his forehead. It was a sign of one of the intense headaches he often got and which I now could anticipate as one would a storm on a tossing sea.

He opened the door and called out into the hallway, "Poli! Poli, you damned fool! Bring me one of your powders!"

Only moments later Polidori reappeared with the "remedy" on a small silver tray. Albé lifted the glass and drank. Suddenly, he spat it on the floor.

"Good God! Are you trying to kill me, man!" he screamed. Then he doubled over in a spasm of pain, Polidori and Shelley immediately to his side and helping him from the room as he retched miserably, a fact that most probably saved his life, for the potion he had taken was poisonous indeed!

We helped him to his bed and Claire brewed him some green tea.

"It was that fool apothecary," Polidori protested as he re-entered the bedroom. "I have just tested it and he sold me some bad magnesia. I have sent a servant to fetch him this very moment."

Albé was too exhausted to speak but he rolled his head to one side, glancing across the room at Polidori, and smiled obliquely as Polidori backed out of the room.

A short time later, the servant returned with the apothecary in tow. Claire and I remained by Albé's bedside but I could hear a terrible row between Polidori and the man and Shelley's voice growing strident, too, as he attempted to put some order to a difficult situation.

I left Claire to tend to Albé and hurried out to the reception room which was on the same floor.

As I entered, Shelley was pulling Polidori away from the grey-headed, bespectacled apothecary, whom Polidori had collared.

"Murderer!" Polidori screamed.

The little man was free and hurried to the door. Shelley immediately unlatched it for him and as Shelley's back was turned and the man unguarded for that instant, Polidori lunged at him, ripped the man's spectacles from his face and before Shelley could stop him, dashed them to the floor and ground them to dust beneath the heel of his well-polished shoe.

The little man shook with fury. "I shall bring you to trial for this," he warned Polidori and then blindly left the room, stumbled down the front stairs and ran down and away through the underbrush.

It was decided that Claire and I should return right away to Chapuis, whilst Shelley remain for a time with Albé. Polidori was not the least bit pleased with this and Claire sulked, having wanted to remain and nurse Albé through the night, if need be. She did, however, sense as I did, that Albé did not care to be alone with Polidori. I doubted if he feared him as I did, for Albé appeared to fear very little save his own tormented memories. But he was, I believed, so thoroughly angry with Polidori that, like the child he often became, he sought instant revenge. Shelley's presence at Diodati that night, when Polidori most needed to reinstate himself in Albé's graces, succeeded immediately in achieving this.

Claire and I walked silently back to Chapuis, where we each went directly to our own room.

I found myself unable to sleep. This was the first night since our elopement that Shelley had not shared our bed. I walked restlessly through all the rooms in which we had walked and sat and spoken together. Shelley . . . Shelley . . . how does one call love? What name can be assigned to the haunting fear that one day that love would pass beyond—was slipping away even now?

I sat down and began to write in my journal as though it were a letter I was writing to Shelley.

Please remember, Shelley, all the nights we spent in each other's arms, with the lake before us and the mighty Jura. These nights will pass, and a time may come when I weep to read these words and Death, too, will at length come. And in the last moment, all will be a dream. But now all is real and you must remember, you must. Oh, dear Shelley, you must.

11

It was a night of very high wind, clouds hurrying over the sky like spilt milk blown out of the pail—rain pelting—lightning flashing and the lake roaring as it lapped the shore, and we had made our way to Chillon in the very thick of it.

We went directly to the dungeons. Shelley and Albé had spent some time alone at Diodati before our departure. I was certain they had taken some laudanum. Shelley's eyes were glassed over and his colour high. I was disturbed but decided I would reserve my censure for later when Shelley and I were alone.

It was cold and damp and we huddled close together in a group, not yet forming Albé's circle. Shelley had one arm about me and was holding a candle with the other and the flames flickered dangerously close to our faces as the wind swept through the dungeons.

:[115]:

Albé had decided this was his night to tell his story, but when we arrived, he said he was not quite ready. He had brought a flask of brandy and each of us took a long drink to warm ourselves.

Fanny had sent on Coleridge's poem *Christabel* and it had arrived that morning and been shared with Albé. What had followed was one of the most unpleasant afternoons I had ever spent.

The poem was about a young woman named *Christabel*, who was born as her mother died and who lived with the ghost of her mother inside her. When she was grown, she met a woman named Geraldine in the forest and brought her home that night to her castle. Geraldine is the evil incarnation of her mother and, before leaving Christabel and her husband in their castle, cast an evil spell upon them.

In itself it was a frightening poem but Albé saw something even deeper and more sinister in it.

"Striking resemblance to your own case, eh, Mary?" he had said, smiling broadly.

"Not in my opinion," I replied coldly.

He had been pacing the room and was behind me so that I had to turn my head awkwardly to see him.

"Why, it is as clear and heavily drawn as Poli's eyebrows on his face! It is no secret your mother died when you were born."

"Twelve days after."

"Little difference. And from all I have heard, you are truly a reincarnation of your mother. Godwin saw to that, bringing you up exactly as she was. Instilling guilts and worse, *passions* in you to be truly her, loving you a bit unnaturally, I would say."

"Quite enough, Albé," Shelley interrupted, anger in his usually gentle eyes.

But Albé came around from behind and now stood between Shelley and myself so that neither of us could see the other. He was speaking over his shoulder to Shelley but his eyes never left my face.

"This is all in the interest of literary knowledge, Shelley," he said. "One must not intrude upon the search for truth in poetry. It helps us to understand the interpretation of our own work—and our own lives." He moved aside then and with a curious sense of rejection, I saw that Shelley's anger had been pacified and his attention and glance were entirely Albé's.

"Coleridge, of course, knows your father," Albé continued, "and, I might add, knew your mother. He spoke of her to me once. She impressed him greatly." He sat down, his cane between his legs, his body resting forward on it, his eyes still locked with mine.

"What do you suppose he is saying in the poem, Mary? I for one have already made my conjecture. He is saying—*Exorcise your mother's ghost or you will destroy Shelley.*" His voice was low and intimate, meant for no one in that room save me and there was a sudden softness in his eyes. Perhaps I am not incorrect in calling it *a plea*.

I sat there, outwardly cold and reserved, but I could hear the sound of my own heartbeat. "I will not listen to such nonsense," I told him plainly. Then I stood up to leave.

"Departing so early? Well, no matter, Shelley and I have things to discuss." He rose and came to my side and took my arm and led me out to the hallway. "We will go to Chillon tonight," he said. "Poli will see you and Claire back to Chapuis and remain with you until Shelley and I join you."

Polidori was not the least bit happy but he did as he was told; I left out of fury, more against myself than at Albé or Shelley, and waited for Shelley's return in extreme agitation, but praying he would return for an evening when we could be together and alone.

Now, here we were a group once again—a spell certainly upon us all, for I had been unable to refuse Albé's command that we come this night to Chillon.

We stood before the Pillar in the shadow of those piercing arches. Our candles formed a circle, but each of us seemed in his own world. I felt bruised and angry. I was here against my true will. I stood beside Shelley. His eyes were glazed and a far-off expression veiled the Shelley I knew. He was in a dream state. (I feared thinking of it as a drugged state, and do even now.)

Albé, as captain of our forces, appeared to change his mind about telling his tale. He stood there smiling in the flickering candlelight. We were all silent and all was silence and darkness about us. Claire trembled and a small sigh was denied life as she held it back. Time passed—but I do not know whether it was seconds or minutes. Then Albé began to recite in his deepest voice of melancholy and foreboding a stanza from *Christabel:*

> *Then drawing in her breath aloud*
> *Like one that shuddered, she unbound*
> *The cincture from beneath her breast;*
> *Her silken robe and inner vest*

Dropt to her feet, and fully in view
Behold! her bosom and half her side,
HIDEOUS, DEFORMED AND PALE OF HUE,
A sight to dream of, not to tell!
AND SHE IS TO SLEEP BY CHRISTABEL.

No one stirred. Something very curious was happening. Darkness and silence surrounded us like a shroud. Even the wind appeared to have lost its voice. Then, slowly, trembling in fear, Shelley's hand drew back and away from me. He took several steps backward, his eyes staring. Albé, who was nearest him, stood away but I, in fear of his condition, in fear of what might happen if I did not—started toward him.

Suddenly he shrieked quite wildly, an animal sound, piercing the unnatural silence that had preceded it, causing my heart and pulse to go wild. But I froze where I was, not daring to move closer, terrified now of what might occur if I did. He was staring at the bodice of my dress as though able to see through the folds of heavy cloth. His breath was heavy, and his eyelids fluttered as though he might faint, but then he turned and, holding the candle high, ran shrieking from the dungeons and out into the cold darkness of the night.

Fearing he would do damage to himself, all of us followed the inhuman sound of his shrieking and the path of flickering light from his candle. He had re-entered the castle and was running through the deserted corridors when suddenly he found Ianthe standing solidly in his pathway. His shriek faded into the wind and his candle fell to the stone floor and he beside it.

Not having water, Polidori dashed brandy on his face

and he came to and began to sob hysterically that he had seen eyes where my nipples should have been. He had seen a pair of staring eyes in my breast—as though another woman lived inside my body—as though I were Christabel.

Polidori then gave him some ether to quiet him down and Claire crouched down beside him to wipe his perspiring brow. I stared accusingly at Albé, but he was joined in another contest with Ianthe.

"Evil," she spat at him. "The very Devil himself!"

"We have had a bit too much to drink. I do apologize for my friends. Poets, I am afraid, were not created to hold their liquor well." He smiled at her, the small boy asking indulgence.

Ianthe did not reply. But she stood there silently until Shelley was capable of being raised to his feet and until we had left Chillon.

There would be no ghost stories this night, but in my heart I knew our own ghosts were already being raised.

12

There is a voice not understood by all . . . .
—SHELLEY, Cancelled passage, Mont Blanc, 1816

Shelley was the elder brother of a troop of small sisters
and as such could have been in his childhood hero or
tyrant to them all. He chose rather to be their companion
and to lead them into regions of imaginary enchantment
and terror. He created great stories of horror for them,
all of them becoming fiends while Shelley would play the
devil. Once he set a stack of wood on fire to create "a
little hell of his own"! His mother was, according to him,
narrow-minded, violent and domineering. She seemed to
have a special grievance against Shelley because he was
not her idea of a country gentleman and because he disliked sports. She made him fish from a boat as she
watched and sent him hunting with the gamekeeper, but

Shelley sat "consorting with ghosts," as he tells it, while the gamekeeper hunted, the dead birds afterwards being presented to Mrs. Shelley as having been shot by Shelley. He always believed in witches and ghosts and legendary miracles, and he claimed his mother believed he was on the high road to Hell and that he wanted to make a deistical coterie of his little sisters.

At a very young age he became an atheist, considering the word "God" a vague word and its continued use injurious to mankind. He did, however, believe in the soul and respected the life of a leaf, of a tree, and of the meanest insect. While at Oxford, he set down these views in a pamphlet called *The Necessity of Atheism*. Shortly afterwards he was sent down and so never did complete his education.

He moved to London and set himself up independently. He was a young man of nineteen, an outcast from Oxford and an exile from his father's house, when he met Harriet. He was most grateful to anyone who would extend friendship to him at that time. Harriet was only sixteen, a friend of one of his sisters. She invited him to dinner and fell instantly in love with him. It was only much later and too late for Harriet to turn back that she discovered Shelley was an atheist. She had not even understood the meaning of that word and when he explained it to her, she had been terrified. She did not see how he could live one moment professing such principles and she refused to listen to his arguments. She believed in eternal punishment and was dreadfully afraid of the Devil. From the day she married Shelley, she lived in terror that if she listened to Shelley, she would be lost to the Devil.

Harriet was, throughout their short marriage, no more than a skittish schoolgirl with no intellectual powers, no resolute will. And so I understood what Shelley loved most in me and what he expected of my love. He had been surrounded all his life either by women who followed him blindly or by women who refused to accept him as he was. I was, therefore, to accept him (as indeed he accepted me) as he was, but not without question or challenge.

We stared at each other now across the length of our bedroom. Shelley was already in bed, and I sat, fully dressed, in the one sturdy chair in the room. For the first time in our relationship, I felt hostility and anger towards him.

"I shall not play the shrew, Shelley. Nothing could make me so humble myself," I said, trying to keep the emotion down in my voice. "Nor will I act the prude. I am not, never have been, and never can conceive of myself being so!—but I fear what you are doing, what we *all* are doing, and I know only you can put a halt to what could possibly end in tragedy!" I bit my lip and held back the bitter words that seemed bound to follow.

"Ah, Mary, the branded lioness leading forth her young to teach them they must forego their inborn thirst of death—" He leaned forward. "But what is death, Mary, but the unknown? And what is there to fear of the unknown once it reveals itself to us? I am searching for truth, for reality—no more, no less."

"Being dead seems real enough to me."

"It is another state. I have always believed that. Science convinces me that must be true. If earth feeds on our bones, we become earth, trees, flowers, the birds, the very air. And then"—he smiled wistfully—"there is the soul."

"It is not death I fear—but reality." I stood up and began to pace back and forth in the small area between the bed and the chair, feeling his eyes on me all the while. "Whatever is beginning to occur among us has its roots in evil. I am possessed with that thought."

"Evil? What is evil, Mary?"

"Sin, then! Sin!" My voice rose and I paused before him. His face never lost its composure, or his voice its calm.

"What sin can there possibly be in searching for truth? There cannot be, Mary, any more than that there could be sin in love."

"In idolatry!"

He smiled. "I idolize you. Is that sinful?"

"I am speaking about his Lordship." I leaned in close to him. The heat was in my cheeks. "He is gaining a command over you. I feel it. I see it. Shelley, listen to me. Lord Byron is a fascinating, faulty, childish, philosophical being—daring the world, impetuous and indolent, gloomy and yet more gay than any other. I can reconcile myself to those waywardnesses which disturb me so because of the excitement he instills in me. I understand you reacting in the same manner. But, recall, as I do, your confiding to me that he is mad as the winds. Would you be an abject follower in madness? Could you be so blind as to link hands with the Devil?"

"Madness, Mary, is all about us. It is the very air we breathe. Should we stop breathing for fear of its exhilaration?"

I sat down on the edge of the bed. I could feel my hand shake and I grasped one with the other and held them firmly in my lap. "You are very often like a small boy, Shelley. You are loath to see wrong in those you love. I admire Lord Byron as you do, though I am convinced you are twice the poet and twice the man he is. I admire him for much the same reasons you do. He is not just a wanderer—he has an aim, a purpose. He is a man in search of the elixir of life. But you have already found your purpose. You, Shelley, are a great poet—someday England's *greatest!* That is your aim—because through your words, political freedom will became a rallying cry to the masses and tyranny and misery and evil will be faced with a mighty foe."

I unclasped my hands and concentrated on smoothing out the folds in my skirt—any activity to keep from looking Shelley in the eye. "I want to leave Switzerland," I said carefully.

"Alone?"

I reacted instinctively, "Of course not. With you!"

"To run away to preserve love is one thing, Mary. To do so to avoid truth, quite another."

"Truth? Truth!" I jumped to my feet. "What truth, Shelley, are you going to find in the use of drugs, in the tracking of ghostly spectres, in the haunting of our hearts? In your poetry, that is where the truth rests."

"But, Mary, I must know it first."

"You do already. Believe me, you do," I pleaded. "It is an instinctive thing with you. The truth breathes in all your poetry, Shelley, as does your struggle not to despair." I wrung my hands as though I were wringing the words from me. Then I came around the bed and grasped hold of the brass foot rail to give me further security.

"I do not like what is happening to me watching you experiment, fearing those stories, these dredgings of our basest emotions. Tonight you feared me. Me, Shelley, ME!" I began to cry and had to turn aside to fight for control.

Shelley rose from the bed hastily and came around it and grasped my shoulders tightly between his hands. He was conscious that I could not look at him at the moment and sensitive enough not to insist I do. "If you gave yourself opportunity to know him better," he began, then he must have felt my body tense for he said no more on that subject and his voice grew tender. "You are so young, Mary. I keep forgetting how young you are. It is seldom that the young know what youth is, till they have got beyond it. Youth, my darling, is the passion you have just displayed."

I turned, still without looking at him, and buried my face in his chest. He stroked my back as he held me tightly to him. "If, Mary, I am to write fearlessly, then I am pledged to live fearlessly. Albé is perhaps in shape a Scaramouche, in hue Othello, but once unveiled—you will see a fellow scorched by Hell but driven by love." He lifted my face now and kissed away my tears. "You will stay here with me, of course."

I nodded my head and he kissed me on the forehead.

"By chance if eyes needs must weep, I could make their tears all wonder and delight," he whispered into my ear. "And change eternal death into a night of glorious dreams so that the living would not be envied by the dead, nor death feared by the living."

He guided me to the side of the bed. "We shall love eternally," he said. Then he grinned. "But first, my love, my very own love, perhaps we should be a bit earthly."

And our argument ended as arguments must between fresh lawn sheets and upon the pillows of desire.

13

As a girl, I lived principally in the country and passed a considerable time in Scotland. Father remained in London on Skinner Street with his new wife and her family whilst I lived with some family friends, the Baxters, until I was a girl in my adolescence. In Scotland I lived on the blank and dreary shores of the Tay, near Dundee. Bland and dreary in retrospect I call them; they were not so to me then. They were the eyrie of freedom and the pleasant region where I could commune with the creatures of my fancy. I wrote then, but in a most commonplace style. It was beneath the trees of the grounds belonging to our house, or on the bleak sides of the woodless mountains near, that my true compositions, the airy flights of my imagination, were born and fostered. I did not make myself the heroine of my tales. Life appeared to me too commonplace an affair. I could

:[129]:

not believe that romantic woes or wonderful events would ever be my lot. But I was not confined to my own identity, and I could people the hours with creations far more interesting to me at that age than my own sensations.

Now life seemed more unreal than any story I could select to write and when each day Lord Byron would ask if I had thought of my story, I would have to reply with a negative. Shelley was most anxious that I begin a literary career and thought this the perfect opportunity. He was forever reminding me of my literary parentage and considered it my duty to obtain my own reputation. But everything must have a beginning, to speak in Sanchean phrase, and the beginning must be linked to something that went before. The Hindus gave the world an elephant to support it, but they made the elephant stand on a tortoise. I had no tortoise yet and so—no story. Yet the stirrings were always with me, and I rose restless in the morning and at night, when at last I would close my eyes, peace eluded me.

It was not just the nameless, unknown terrors that unnerved me, it was the reality of what was happening back in England as well. Daily, Shelley and I received letters pertaining to Harriet's condition, for she appeared to be on the very edge of madness and despair and her father and sister were convinced that she would end a harlot on the streets or a madwoman in debtors' prison. Letters from my sister Fanny also conveyed despair for my father's solvency and mental balance. Shelley's desertion of their cause had cut him deeply. Greater truth, perhaps, was the lack of funds Shelley's dereliction had created. Father claimed, Fanny wrote, that Shelley had promised him, earlier in the year, three hundred pounds and that he had acted accordingly and had indebted himself for that amount and now did not have the funds to cover. So there was Father to worry about. *And Fanny.* Fanny whom I loved more than any other person save Shelley. Older than myself, unmarried, sensible and sensitive—*Fanny.* Orphaned, yet legally adopted by my father, we were more of a piece than Claire and myself, having had the same mother. As Claire relied upon me, so I had relied upon Fanny. I had had small guilt about deserting Father because I knew Fanny was at home to cope with the situation and to stand by his side. But Fanny's letters now showed a despondency for herself I had not previously been aware existed.

And so I was torn daily by remorse and despair and woke each morning in horror that what was happening in England was the work of my own hands.

These were things I did not confide in Shelley. Indeed, I confided in no one and so all the unspoken words, the unspent emotion became imprisoned in my crowded heart.

The morning after what I have come to think of as *the first confrontation* was brazen and gold and unafraid. It announced itself early on as heralding a clear, warm summer's day.

Shelley decided the two of us should go on an outing alone, and so I packed a lunch for us and we departed before Claire had awakened.

On the crest of the small mountain behind Chapuis and overlooking the lake, there was an old, deserted village (so our manservant informed us) dating from the thirteenth century. On first seeing the crumbling fortress wall from the shore, I thought immediately of a feudal lord protecting his tribe from any and all strangers from the sea.

We decided that we would ascend the mountain to the crest, if at all possible, and have a look around. Shelley had a telescope with him and we both wore suitable shoes for climbing.

The ascent was precipitous. However, sunlight splashed our path and the trail itself was cut into continual and short windings which enabled us to progress upward without too much concern. The pines were not tall or luxuriant. They were, in fact, quite sombre and lent an air of severity to the climb. We were both in high spirits, though, the healing warmth of the day, the exertion of the climb, all added to a sense of mounting enthusiasm to reach the summit. As we went higher, there were trees broken and strewn on the ground, some entirely destroyed, others bent, leaning upon the jutting rocks of the mountain or across other trees—all traces of a winter avalanche.

Shelley and I rested on a rock that must have rolled with the avalanche as well. We had been climbing for two hours and the crest remained about an hour's climb above. We ate our lunch and then stretched out on top of the rock with a half-bent pine branch for shade. I could feel the happiness creeping back into my body. It was a joyous feeling and Shelley saw it in the smile I could not suppress.

I heard Shelley's soft words in my ear as though a gentle breeze carried them. "I vow to dedicate my powers to thee, Mary, and thine. And call the phantoms of a thousand hours spent with thee as witness to my vow."

I opened my eyes. Shelley lay beside me, his eyes searching out my response.

I took his outstretched hand. "Love me tenderly, Shelley," I said clearly, "as I vow always to love thee."

"I worship thee, Mary—Mary—" He raised his lean body and arched it over me, his golden hair catching the rays of sun sifting through the leaves above us, and sealed our marriage with a kiss that was a pledge and I returned his pledge for my own.

We lay there then side by side and touching, not speaking, listening to a leaf in the soft wind, an insect beneath a rock, a bird perched on a limb. We listened to the clock of nature, listened as time passed.

Then for a moment, *minutes*, neither of us were aware of which, we rose from the altar of our vows and hand in hand set out to reach the summit. The path was smoother near the top, rocks had rolled down and cleared the brush. I was, however, experiencing an exaltation that had more to do with the emotion I felt towards Shelley than the rarity of the air or the labour of the climb. Shelley now walked before me smiling back at me every so often, but our climb was a silent one. Yet, afterwards, both of us confided that never had our communication been so intense.

We came first upon an ancient graveyard, small, most graves unmarked, the others bearing only small stone crosses. But it was not neglected and looked as though someone had, in fact, tended it recently. The wall had been destroyed by the heavy snows of the previous winter and so by standing on the edge of the graveyard one had the feeling of nothing at all holding you back from the deep chasm of dark shadow below. I stood with an incredible fascination staring down so that Shelley finally, fearing I might accidentally slip, drew me away from the edge and in doing so lost his telescope, which he had been holding. We stood watching as it rolled down the side of the steep slope until it was entirely vanished from our sight.

"It was something you prized and it was my fault," I said, near tears. "I cannot bear the thought of my causing you the loss of any dear thing," I whispered.

"I prize nothing more than you," he replied and smiled. I smiled back but nonetheless, the incident was the first blot upon the most beautiful day thus far in my life.

There was an arch hewn from rock that separated the graveyard from the village and we passed beneath it having to bend in half to clear the wild overhang of brush that had blocked our sight of the village.

Once on the other side we stood—afraid to move, afraid our footsteps would disturb the incredible stillness that now surrounded us.

The village was mostly destroyed, but the narrow cobblestoned streets remained and sections of stone houses, and a place was marked where a fountain and a square had been—and beyond was the façade of a tiny church with what appeared to be a fresh cross over its door.

There was the sound of a church bell, dissident, badly out of tune, coming from behind the façade which was all of the church that appeared to be standing.

Shelley pulled me forward but I walked fearfully behind him as he headed for the church. Obstinately, he would not enter through the front door and beneath the cross. Instead, we circled the building and approached it from the side. Someone had been trying to rebuild it with small stones, and by hand. Shelley lifted me up and over the newer section of the wall and then followed.

The floor was still dirt but there was an altar and across the expanse of the open room was a priest laboriously polishing a huge church bell. He had not heard us and did not see us for a long time as he was so very engrossed in his work. I wanted to leave then, not to interrupt or to intrude, but Shelley drew me forward with him. Our shadows fell across the priest's path. He looked up and, squinting from the sun behind us for a moment, seemed attempting to recognize us and then, finally, accepting us as strangers, he got to his feet.

"Have you come to pray?" he asked, in a strange dialect of French that I could only barely comprehend.

"We are sorry to have intruded," Shelley told him. But the priest did not seem to understand. He came closer to us.

"This is a church. You are welcome. But you must pray," I thought he said.

Shelley seemed to interpret the man's words the same way. "I am sorry," he repeated and then, taking my hand, began to walk towards the door. There he paused.

"I have not advanced this far to pass beneath the sign of the cross," he said and turned aside and walked back to the half-built wall once again, lifted me over and then himself. The sun was going down. There would only be about three hours until darkness set in. Shelley hurried me back across the crumbling village and drew me under the archway to the graveyard and made his way quickly past its freshly blessed graves as I followed. There were violet and golden pansies growing in profusion and we paused among them.

"Pansies are for memory," he said and, bowing low, gently plucked a richly coloured one and gave it solemnly to me. I stared upon its face and his. Both were smiling wistfully. Then he turned and we began the descent that would take us back to Chapuis, and as we did, the bell began to toll again. That sound was to remain in my ears that night, and for many nights to come. This was the 29th of July and I would always consider it the day Shelley and I were united.

14

But first, on earth as Vampyre sent,
Thy corse shall from its tomb be rent;
Then ghastly haunt thy native place,
And suck the blood of all thy race;
There from thy daughter, sister, wife,
At midnight drain the stream of life;
Yet loathe the banquet which perforce
Must feed thy livid living corse.
—LORD BYRON, *The Giaour*, 1813

Albé had first had the ghoulish legend of the vampyre on his mind when he wrote this verse for *The Giaour* in the spring of '13, over three years earlier. The superstition of the dead rising from their graves and feeding upon the blood of the young and beautiful was Eastern in derivation, but is spread, with some slight variation, all over Hungary, Poland, Austria and Lorraine, where the belief extended that vampyres nightly drained a certain portion of the blood of their victims, who then became emaciated, lost their strength and speedily died of consumption; whilst these human blood suckers fattened—their veins becoming so distended as to flow from all the passages of their bodies and even from the very pores of their skin.

The London *Journal*, of March, 1732 (according to Albé who had done considerable research on the subject) actually carried a credible account of a particular case of vampyrism, which is stated to have occurred in Hungary. It appears that upon an examination of the commander-in-chief and magistrates of the place, they positively and unanimously affirmed that about five years before a man had claimed he had been tormented by a vampyre but had found a way to rid himself of the evil by eating some of the earth out of the vampyre's grave and rubbing himself with its blood. This precaution, however, did not prevent him from becoming a vampyre himself, and for about twenty or thirty days after his death and burial, many persons complained of having been tormented by him, and a deposition was made that four persons had been deprived of life by his attacks. To prevent further mischief, the inhabitants, having consulted their chief bailiff, took up the body and found it, as is supposed to be usual in cases of vampyrism, fresh, and entirely free from corruption, and emitting at the mouth, nose and ears pure and florid blood. Proof having been thus obtained, they resorted to the accustomed remedy. A stake was driven entirely through the heart and body of the vampyre, at which he is reported to have cried out as dreadfully as if he had been alive. This done, they cut off his head, burned his body and threw the ashes into his grave. The same measures were adopted in the cases of the corpses of his victims, lest they should, in their turn, become agents preying upon others who survived them.

There is a further superstition that for a sort of punishment after death for some heinous crime committed whilst in existence the deceased would not only be doomed to vampyrise, but be compelled to confine his infernal visitations to those beings he loved most whilst upon earth—those to whom he was bound by strongest ties of kindred and affection.

It was this that had been alluded to by Albé in *The Giaour.*

> *There from thy daughter, sister, wife,*
> *At midnight drain the stream of life;*
> *Yet loathe the banquet which perforce*
> *Must feed thy livid living corse.*

The night Albé selected to tell his story, he refused to have us leave for Chillon before the stroke of midnight.

The sky was swept with shadow and the moon was lost from sight. I could see only the darkened, misshapen forms of the mountains lurking like some sullen, brooding beasts in the distance and then, again, seeming only darker patches of the night.

By the time we reached Chillon it was that hour of the night that is the stillest. Cottages no longer showed light. The sounds of the night creatures echoed in our ears louder than our own heartbeats. For the world of dark blue and shadow was their world, not ours.

Polidori had brought along the stringed instrument he often played as we travelled, he plucked at it, its notes dispelling gloom. Still, none of us heeded its sound, for each seemed to be self-involved. Yet, do not let me create the false illusion that a dismal and melancholy mood prevailed upon us. On the contrary! Albé appeared quite high-spirited and as we moved through the blindfold of night, he would laugh suddenly at some private thought or wandering idea. He had one arm wrapped about Claire and she leaned maidenlike against him, smiling contentedly. Shelley was dreaming poet's dreams, looking out to the unseeable as though he could, in fact, see the crest of Mount Olympus. And I—Ah! Well, that is another matter! I sat impatiently, chafing, my indignation stifled by my refusal to ruffle my outward dignity and appear for all to see—a sullen woman, flushed with rage and about to fly into a temper. For laudanum had been taken by all save me before departure.

Though Albé might call me a prude, narrow-minded—and a bore—I knew he actually admired my strong nature and, though he did all he could to taunt me into submission, would have been gravely disappointed had he been able to succeed.

It is not easy to remain the odd one out. More difficult still when it was not that you simply disapproved of what your companions were doing, but rather that you felt them and yourself capable of such a higher level of experimentation. The use of an artificial stimulant already conceded one's creativity deficient, lacking, unable to perform without aid. But I had pledged to myself that though I would not partake with them, neither would I censure them for their participation.

We went directly to the dungeons, single file as always, Albé leading, our candles high. As we entered the giant arches all seemed like ghostly arms raised, hands interlocked. No moonlight could be seen and the quiet was awesome.

Albé stood with his back to the Prisoner's Pillar. "Tonight, I shall relate the horrific tale of a vampyre condemned in death for life's sins to suck the blood of his dearest, closest kin," he announced.

He was holding his candle with his right hand and he raised his left in signal and bowed his head. Slowly we all lowered ourselves to the cold stone floor. He stood still, glancing down at us. He opened wide his left hand and we placed our candles before us.

"Join hands," he said softly.

We did as he said, excluding him from our circle. Shelley and my hands crossed before him and locked, barring him, setting him apart. I clasped hands with Claire who sat on the other side of me. Polidori was between Shelley and Claire.

Albé remained standing as he began to recite from his own poem in a voice of *deathly cold!*

> *"Thou must end thy task and mark*
> *Her cheek's last tinge—her eye's last spark,*
> *And the last glassy glance must view*
> *Which freezes o'er its lifeless blue;*
> *Then with unhallowed hand shall tear*

:[141]:

The tresses of her yellow hair,
Of which in life a lock when shorn
Affection's fondest pledge was worn—
But now is borne away by thee
Memorial of thine agony!
Yet with thine own best blood shall drip,
Thy gnashing tooth and haggard lip;
Then stalking to thy sullen grave,
Go—and with Gouls and Afrits rave,
Till these in horror shrink away
From spectre more accursed than they.''

And then he began his story. But I shall have to tell it as I saw it then—for saw it, I did, as though the drama had come to life before my eyes. Undrugged, sober, conscious all the while—and yet, what I am about to relate will, I know, seem to you a nightmare of madness.

15

It came with the wind first, as the candle flickered and as I watched the mesmerizing flame and as Albé's compelling voice filled my consciousness. *The first image*. It slithered from the candle as a snake might, from the brightness of the flame to the grey-black of its smoke, to the upper regions of darkness—from day and twilight—to night. Albé's voice now an echoing thunder and the flame reflections like blue forked lightning seeming to fall at the image's feet. *The image*. A formless, creeping thing, bearing only one discernible feature—Albé's maleficent eyes, pitiless, implacably staring at me.

"A young man named Aubrey," the voice inside my head was saying, "came beneath the vampyre's curse and so feared the cursed destruction of the one he loved most, that he deserted his homeland and wandered to far and distant shores. Lonely, ever lonely, he was the dark figure on a black horse riding through eternal night. One night storms and heavy rains forced him into a dense and entangled forest where he came upon an apparently deserted hut.

"He dismounted and approached, hearing the cry of a woman mingled with the mockery of exultant laughter. He was startled and hesitated, for the laughter seemed to be issuing from himself. But then the thunder rolled again and he forced himself to approach the door of the hut."

The image was not far from me now. I felt its cold breath on my bared neck and could see the insulting laughter in those eyes. My hands were chained to either side of me and I was unable to raise my scarf to bind and protect my exposed flesh. I was aware of no one else. Only *the image*, which now drew away and back into the darkness, eluding my sight but not my presentiment of its ever-presence—and the voice—*the voice* continued within my head.

"Aubrey forced open the door. He found himself in utter darkness and there were sounds from its depth. He called. No one replied. He began to advance towards the sounds, into the very eye of the dark. A woman was sobbing. At last, his hand touched flesh and incredibly, a strength matching his own, a strength not given to women, struggled against him. He felt himself being lifted and hurled with enormous force upon the floor of the hut. He recalled stumbling to his feet, remembered dimly making his way back through the room and flinging the door wide as he fell onto the masses of dead leaves that surrounded the hut.

"Aubrey was incapable of moving. Torchlight burst upon him. There surrounding him was a circle of strangers holding their torches high. One man held in his arms no torch but the form of the lifeless corpse of a young woman—Aubrey's bride.

"There was no colour in her cheeks, or upon her lip, yet there was a stillness about her face that seemed almost as attaching as the life that once dwelt there . . . and Oh!—Lord! . . . upon her neck and breast was blood and upon her throat were the marks of teeth across the vein. New cries now filled Aubrey's head.

" 'A vampyre! A vampyre!' the men shouted pointing with terror at the corpse's neck.

"Aubrey drew his dagger and held it tightly to him, waiting for the right moment and praying he would be able to drive it accurately through his own heart.

"He watched them as they laid his loved one on the dead leaves beside him and as they formed a litter. To his shock, they then lifted both of them upon the litter and carried them through the forest.

"You see, he was dead, but he did not know it. For it was still night, the time when vampyres stalk. He was now ghoul, not man. And he had been condemned to stalk the nights of eternity as he would the one person in all the world he had loved the most."

The voice had ceased but the image drew close to me. It was gone from my sight but it was there directly behind me. I wanted to move. Then I felt a pressure on my back and I screamed until I felt my blood fill my brain and my throat grow raw.

I recall Albé's penitent face above mine. "It was only my hand, Mary," he was saying. "My hand upon your neck. I was behind you and lowering myself to the ground."

I nodded my head so that he would know I understood, but I was unable to speak. Shelley lifted me in his arms and carried me into the night air and rested me against the steps of the dungeon. He was speaking gently, soothing me, reassuring me, but I could not hear anything he said, for the voice was still continuing in my head—Albé's voice—undeniably Albé's voice:

"A vampyre, was there ever so accurate a portrait of your Lordship as a ghoul doomed to stalk the night, cursed to destroy whomever he loves most."

And then, strangely, I thought I heard the sound of Albé's laughter.

16

The next day I woke exhausted and alone. Shelley had left me a note saying that both he and Claire had already gone up to Diodati. As it was not many minutes past midday, I hurriedly dressed to join them. It was unusual for Albé to be awake so early, more unusual yet for Shelley to join Claire in her afternoon visit.

When I arrived, Polidori greeted me and wasted no time in telling me, with great irritation, that Albé, Shelley and Claire had closed themselves in the library, barring his entrance.

"Has anything unforeseen happened?" I asked with alarm.

"Hardly unforeseen. You would not recall I am sure, all that took place last night," he said, "but Claire did not return to Chapuis. No, the dear little lady spent the night here. No one got any sleep, I might add. My eyelids need propping, I am so damned fatigued. She talked all night—all morning! His Lordship has not slept an hour for her incessant harping."

"Harping?"

"First she seemed concerned that our harmless experiments might be injurious to her condition. I am sure you know about her *condition?*"

"If you mean that Claire is with child, yes, I know that, of course."

"*With child.* How charmingly put." Polidori removed a vial from his pocket and, taking a pill from it, slipped it into his mouth. "I shall never last the day," he said.

I had crossed to the door of the library and stood unsure of whether to knock or not.

"I have seen less concern outside operating theatres," Polidori remarked.

"Some people are born to cope. Claire is not one of them."

"Not cope—our little Claire? You make me laugh with your naïveté! She has certainly coped very well so far! She knew what she wanted—*our* Claire. And she has copiously succeeded in stalking, luring, seducing and temporarily entrapping his Lordship!" He sat down and smiled insolently up at me. "It is quite obvious really that if she could have had Shelley, she would have done. That sort of rivalry occurs often between sisters. But you would have been a formidable force for Claire to overpower and so—whom else—but England's other great poet—England's other scandal. Lord Byron." He breathed deeply. "Vanity! One would not suspect it in one so clever as his Lordship. But she seduced him. Clever bitch. His Lordship has gone into the greatest details . . . . "

"Do be quiet!" I drew back from the door and stood awkwardly, trying to keep my glance away from Polidori.

"You surprise me. The daughter of the great woman's liberator? You—the disciple of all the freedoms—speech, I assume, being among them?" He stood up and came over to me, forcing me to answer his mockery with my own defiance. He seemed suddenly to sober a bit, his face clouding, his voice lowering. "All right, I grant you, our fluttering Claire is a tender creature. Weak—ah, yes!— Weak! But, dear lady, spare me the terrible strength of the weak!"

We stood facing each other. There was shadow darkening his complexion and he was suddenly old.

"What brought Shelley here at so early an hour?" I asked quietly.

"Claire, most naturally. She went to fetch him. They are discussing the child's future. It appears the dear girl cannot exist one more day without matters being settled."

The door from the library opened then and Albé, his face strained, but his eyes flashing, stood angrily for a moment and then noticing me, his attitude changed. He spoke to me curtly, but nonetheless I had the feeling he was glad to see me. "Oh, Mary," he said, "come in, come in."

I could see Claire's pale form behind him and Shelley by her side. He closed and secured the door after us, locking Polidori out. Claire came over and grasped my hand. She said nothing, but her eyes were welling with tears and her hand trembled slightly.

"Claire," Albé called, really a command.

Claire drew away from me and turned to face him. I

sat down and tried to absorb what I could from Shelley's concerned face, his attitude as he leaned against the mantlepiece, Claire's agitation, Albé's directness.

"You knew from the very start I was married," Albé was saying to Claire.

"In your past that has not been an obstacle."

"Nor perhaps in the future. But at this moment, it is."

"I see," Claire said petulantly.

"Umm," Albé sighed. "Dimly, however, and always without foresight."

Shelley straightened. He took a step towards Albé. "Gentler, Milord," he said.

There was silence for a moment or two and then Albé's face softened and he came closer to Claire. "I do not want you to think unkindly of me," he said. "Believe me, I have cared . . . and, in spite of my caustic tongue, I feel tenderly towards you even now." His hand reached out and brushed Claire's cheek. "You have not been unloved. You are not *now* unloved, Claire."

Emotion did not rest easy with Albé and he lowered his hand with some embarrassment to his side and turned, seeming to study a portrait of a sullen young man that hung between two far windows. But if one was close enough, one could see how distracted he was at that moment.

Shelley, it appeared, was playing the mediator. "We are not here to discuss your separate futures," he said, "but to deal with the matter of Claire's confinement and the child's future."

"I will, of course, be responsible for all costs," Albé said in a clear voice.

"I am not a parcel to be dealt with in this way!" Claire

was fighting sobs and I stood instantly and went to her side, which seemed to give her small courage at least and she was able to gain control of herself.

"I am sure Albé only meant to reassure," Shelley began.

But Albé interrupted. "However indelicate, Claire, money at times does have to be pledged verbally." He turned then to Shelley. "I bear all costs," he repeated and there was no questioning the pledge in his voice.

Claire moved to the window, looking out and away, over the gardens, the vineyards and to the lake beyond and the mountains beyond that. Her back was to us all, her head high, her shoulders, though trembling, braced. The two men exchanged glances. Both of them were moved by Claire's situation. Albé sat down and there was another silence before he spoke again.

"We are adults. Our future is in our own hands but the child—that is another matter. It shall, if you permit, Claire, be placed when weaned, in my sister Augusta's care and be raised as a true sister to Medora."

Claire whirled to face Albé. Her shoulders drew back and anger flashed in her eyes and her voice. "No! No! I shall not. Not *her!*"

Albé smiled nervously. "Your determination amazes me, my dear. I would not have thought you would have placed your reputation in such jeopardy, to keep a bastard child by your side."

"*Your* bastard child!" Claire raised her voice and stood almost arrogantly before him.

"I am aware," Albé smiled again, "and not altogether displeased. *My* bastard child—but the world does not have to know it is a bastard or, for the time, my child. It could for all intents and purposes be the child of Augusta's servant, if you prefer."

"*No!*"

For the first time I spoke up. "A child should have its parents' care and love," I said evenly.

"I will take the child to live with me then," Albé said. He did not wait for a reaction from any of us.

"Is there no alternative, Albé?" Claire asked softly.

"It is quite a sensible arrangement, Claire," he replied. "You could visit the child regularly, as though you were—her aunt, a dear friend—and there would be no injury therefore to the child's or to your reputation. And I could be assumed to be the child's guardian."

No one considered how ludicrous that last might appear to the society who considered him England's greatest scandal. All of us were relieved that an amicable solution had been found at least for the time, as Claire could only welcome a *link* that would maintain her relationship with Albé in the future. But pain crossed Claire's face.

"I am certain you will do your duty to the child," she said in a pinched voice, "but love, your Lordship—will you truly extend the child love?"

"Love!" he replied sharply, "I must steel my heart against any love that would rule me, not that which I rule."

"Then my paramount fear must be if the child be loving and you beloved," Claire said in a voice of pure anguish.

"I will, as I stated, do my duty by the child. But do not speak to me of love—the tyrant, the fanged snake. I will have nothing to do with that love, even for a child of my flesh."

"But you will care tenderly for the child?" Claire asked in an anguished voice.

"I vow to that," Albé replied without hesitation.

"Is it agreed then?" Shelley asked Albé.

"With you as my witness," he replied.

"Claire?"

Claire waited, her timing staged, her acting instinct infallible, and when she spoke there was just the right tremour in her voice. "Agreed," she said, "with you, dear Shelley, as my witness." She trembled and for a moment it seemed she might very well faint. Then she turned defiantly to Albé.

He crossed as though to kiss her on the cheek, but Claire slipped past him and to my side. There were great hollows about her eyes, and her skin had no colour at all. I thought, *Claire is only eighteen. All of us must remember she is only eighteen.* And I went before her and opened the door and the two of us left the room together.

Polidori had given up his vigil and appeared to be nowhere about. Albé and Shelley joined us in the reception room and Albé poured us all some claret and we drank it quietly, each of us contained in our own thoughts. Then Albé put down his glass. "I am quite worn out," he said. "I have had no sleep at all." He made to leave the room. "Thank you, Shelley," he said. Then there was the sound of his tired limp on the old wood flooring of the outside hallway.

I had just gone to help Claire with her wrap when we

heard a great commotion coming from the direction of Albé's bed chamber.

When we reached the opened doorway to his room, Albé was grasping Polidori tightly at the throat and was in very close and menacingly to him. It looked as though he might be considering strangling him, and the fear in Polidori's face seemed to assure us that Polidori, at least, thought him capable. Shelley ran over to the men and pulled them apart—with difficulty, as Albé was half-frenzied.

"You want to know my secret thoughts, Poli?" he screamed. "The inner machinations of the scandalous Lord Byron? Revealments to shock and tantalize? A journal you could incorporate with your own? A manuscript that would make you a published author?" He bent over to retrieve the pages of his journal that Polidori had most obviously been reading when Albé had entered the room moments before and which were strewn all over the floor. "You make my flesh crawl, Poli," he hissed. The room was fairly dark, the drapes being still partially closed from night. Albé flung them back and opened the windows wide.

"There is a dark pall—a vulture's shadow—in this room," he said. Then he walked back to his dresser and splashed some water on his face as though needing to wake himself.

"I have been meaning to tell you," Polidori was saying smoothly. "Murray offered me five hundred pounds for your secrets." There was a sense of pride in his arrogant voice.

Albé wiped his face and threw the towel carelessly down on the floor.

"My *own* publisher! How extraordinary! Well, I'll tell you, Poli, if you send one word relating to me to Murray, I swear I shall have your life!"

"You have it already, your Lordship," Polidori quickly replied.

"Get out!" Albé ordered.

There was a long, tense moment, for Polidori did not move. Albé at last turned away and sat down wearily in a chair. "You are a bloodsucker, Poli," he said quietly. "A vampyre. A bloody vampyre."

"And a very good story your vampyre is!" Polidori exclaimed.

"Yes? You think so?" Albé laughed harshly. "Take *that* then, Poli. I give it to you."

"The story of the vampyre?" Polidori inquired, not sure he had heard correctly.

"Yes, *yes*! See what Murray will give you on *that*!"

We withdrew from the room then. Claire was now totally composed.

"Let us go home," she said and then when we were out into the bright day, "*I hate that man! I hate him!*" She began to run down the path towards Chapuis.

"Vampyre!" She was crying into the soft wind. "Vampyre!"

She meant Polidori, of course. I was sure of it. Still, I never inquired of Claire, because we never discussed the events of that day again.

17

To Byron

O Mighty mind, in whose deep stream this age
Shakes like a reed in the unheeding storm,
Why dost thou curb not thine own sacred rage.
—S<small>HELLEY</small>, Summer, 1816

We did not see Albé and Polidori that evening. Instead, Claire and I gathered round Shelley as he read and translated *Prometheus* of Aeschylus. Shelley was very intrigued with the Prometheus story. He was not writing then, but I sensed that he was planning a drama based on the Prometheus legend. He spoke about this possibility, but seemed unable yet to find the proper framework.

I told no one about the apparition I had seen the night

previous, but when Shelley had done reading, we talked of ghosts. We all agreed in the face of reason that none could believe in ghosts without also believing in God, and agreed as well that many who discredit these visitations do not truly discredit them at all or, if they do in the daylight, with the approach of loneliness and midnight think more respectably of the world of shadows.

Shelley considered ghosts a case of mind over matter. Or, in other words, thought projections crystallized so clearly that our mind develops them into images which are projected through our eyes and seen by us in turn.

I went to bed with that thought impressed upon my mind and attempted, in light of it, to analyze my own supernatural experience, but I fell asleep before coming to any acceptable conclusions.

That next night we journeyed once more to Chillon. It was Polidori's turn to be ghost-teller. I had never seen him happier. He sat cross-legged before the Prisoner's Pillar, a smile held to his face only by the fortitude of his small flat ears.

Our candles were lit, our hands were joined. I faced Albé and stared into his eyes. They were not the same eyes of *the image* I had seen the night before. These eyes were still undelivered from pain. These eyes were unforgiving but not maleficent.

"My story," Polidori began, "is a continuation of the story of the vampyre begun two nights ago and thought to be completed—but such was not the case. For you see, the vampyre can never truly be done, for it continues as the life cycle itself. Now, in our story, young Aubrey was

a vampyre—sucked by whom? Perhaps his mother whilst
Aubrey was still in her womb. Who knows? Aubrey, of
course. But Aubrey will never speak."

Albé had closed his eyes and I was not sure if he could
hear or was listening, or was still among us.

"Shall I refresh your memory concerning the vampyre
legend? Yes, I believe I must! The curse as I said, was
never-ending and once a person was sucked by a vampyre, he became a vampyre himself—*and worse yet*, if he
had committed such inexpiable crimes whilst living, was
doomed to vampyrise only those he had loved most on
earth. And the one Aubrey loved most was his sister, the
beauteous, ravishing, seductive *Miss Aubrey.*"

Albé opened his eyes with a start. "Damn you,
Polidori!" he shouted and attempted to rise to his feet,
but Polidori held him on one side and Claire on the other
and he was unable to move.

"It is my turn," Polidori said sharply. "We have all
agreed it is my turn. And, everyone here has witnessed
the fact that you gave me the story. It is now mine to tell
and to embellish as I see fit."

"Damn you," Albé said quietly but harshly and then
closed his eyes again, but this time as though they were
steel gates, prison doors.

"Let us see—Miss Aubrey—Miss Aubrey—Oh, yes!
You see the point is—that is the *omission*—*was*—that
the young damsel who Aubrey vampyrised was *his sister*,
the person he loved most, the person whom he had
deserted his homeland to protect, but the person whom
he must destroy to live.

"As my story opens, Aubrey has sucked his sister's

blood and now she is the vampyre and as her crime, after all, was as heinous as his, perhaps more so, my story is then about Miss Aubrey—The Vampyre."

This time Albé flung out his arms in fury, and as Polidori was grasping him tightly, Polidori's arm as well. A candle went over and Polidori broke away from Albé and stood up quickly to avoid the flame which was dangerously close to his leg. Albé jumped to his feet and, lunging· at Polidori, threw him back against the Prisoner's Pillar. A small wound opened on Polidori's head and the blood trickled down the side of his frightened face.

"Damn you! Damn you!" Albé screamed.

We were all on our feet and Shelley hurried to pull Albé away from Polidori but there was no need. Albé let go his hold and stepped away, some drops of blood from Polidori's wound on the back of his hand. He pushed Shelley aside and then started out of the dungeons. Shelley was soon on one side of him and Claire on the other and they went out into the night.

I wiped the blood from Polidori's wound and doctored it for him with his own tinctures. He was silent, morose. I had never seen him like this before. There was no sullenness, no petulance. He seemed at that moment a man without hope, a man who knows no future.

"Here, Polidori," I said when his wound was tended, "lean on me."

"No, thank you," he said rather humbly and then insisted I go first, which I did.

I joined the others and we waited a few moments for Polidori. As he finally stepped out into the night, he was smiling weakly. Albé and he exchanged neither words nor glances. I assumed he had taken something to lift his spirits. His step was surer. But that was all. Something had died for Polidori only moments before and by his own hand.

I prayed as we left Chillon that night that we might never return. It was one of the many unanswered prayers in my life.

18

. . . the dead! They rise in their shrouds, and pass in silent procession towards the far land of their doom—their bloodless lips move not—their shadowy limbs are void of motion. While still they glide on.

— MARY SHELLEY, *The Last Man*

We had not seen Ianthe this last tortured night in Chillon but now it came to us that her eyes had followed our every move. It did not surprise me for eyes seemed always to be watching from Chillon's dark recesses and I had come to believe that Ianthe was the very darkness itself. I never entered the castle that I did not feel her breath with the opening and closing of each door. Ianthe, so dark, possessed by ages past and voices of the dead— mysterious Ianthe—who walked with lurking shadows, her every step insinuating despair. To think of her filled me more with sadness than with fear.

Lord Byron had no such compassion for her. "Bitch!" he muttered, the next afternoon as I entered the library at Diodati. I stood startled and alone before him. "Ianthe," he explained. "She has been writing letters to the Governor."

"What does she say?"

He angrily ripped a page he was grasping in his hand into bits and tossed them into the flames in the hearth. "What can her words matter?" he said, yet, he stood and watched until each scrap was charred to ash.

"Where are the others?" I inquired.

"Gone for a walk. They will return shortly." He looked up at me now as though only then making note that I had stepped into the room. "Where have you been till now?"

"Delayed by some letters that required my immediate reply." I was uncertain whether I should remain or if I should go out in search of Shelley.

"Sit down," he said, so kindly that I had to comply. "I have been wanting words with you," he said.

"Yes, your Lordship?"

"*Albé.*"

I tried to ease myself into the chair and to smile no matter how faintly. "Albé," I repeated after him.

"Have you no diminutive?"

I laughed uneasily. "Shelley at times calls me the *Maie.*"

He said nothing, but his eyes never left my face. My heartbeat quickened. "I am terribly ill at ease when alone with you," I said forthrightly.

"Were you with Hogg?"

"He has no relevance here."

"Shelley has confided that you were once a *ménage à trois*. Is that correct?"

"If Shelley confided such in you, it would seem honour should bind you to keep that confidence."

"But it is true?"

"One might interpret our relationship so. Shelley and I were both very fond of Hogg and he of each of us. There was nothing secret or underhanded about the affair. Shelley approved of my friendship with Hogg, knew that he made love to me and that I attempted to return his love. I could not because I was and am and shall always be in love with Shelley alone. There can be no possibility in such an experiment occurring again, for Shelley and I are now united as one, which we truly were not at that time."

"I see."

"I trust you truly do."

He crossed over to the window and stood searching the denseness of the late grey afternoon.

"You care very little for women as people and in-dividuals."

He turned slightly but he was standing in the shadows and I could only discern his rigid silhouette.

"I see them as very pretty but inferior creatures," he said, "who are as little in their place at our table as they would be in our council chambers. I look upon them as grown-up children but, like a foolish mama, I am constantly the slave of one of them."

"Even now?"

"Constantly. No, not Claire," he said, as if in answer to my thoughts. "The Turks shut up their women and are now much happier."

"If delusion may be called happiness."

He stepped out of the shadows and closer to me. "I cannot make up my mind whether women have souls but

:[165]:

my *beau idéal* would be a woman with talent enough to understand and value mine, but not sufficient to be able to shine herself."

"That would be as great a delusion as the Turks', Milord, for certainly a woman with that great talent would necessarily shine in her own right."

He smiled bitterly. "Well, you know now where Shelley and I both stand in regard to women. I see them as a pretext for idleness and Shelley sees them as a source of exaltation."

I waited a very long time before speaking my mind. "You may not exaggerate, Milord, when speaking about yourself, but I am not at all certain you always speak the truth."

He turned back into the shadows. "Have you your story yet?" he asked sharply.

"No. I am afraid I have not."

"Have you been giving thought to it?"

"A great deal."

"Why does it seem so difficult?" he inquired, as he once more glanced away from the window and studied me.

"Perhaps, because it matters."

"Yes, I understand that."

"It has been occupying much of my time though. Each day I endeavour to write but cannot. I take solitary walks, or hide myself in my room, my reveries like lions in a tower, but the story will not reveal itself."

He was silent as he studied me. Yet it seemed I heard his words before he spoke.

"Come, sit at my desk," he said to me.

Slowly I rose and crossed the room, conscious each

step of his eyes upon me. It had grown warm in the room and my body felt the heat. When I reached the desk he had paper and pen ready for me, and was standing by my side.

"Now sit down and take the pen in your hand and write."

"What should I write?" I asked, my hand trembling above the sheet of fine parchment.

"When were you born?"

"The thirtieth of August."

"Write it down."

I leaned forward and wrote: *I was born on the thirtieth day of August . . . .*

"Continue," he said as though he were a music teacher and I practising on a keyboard.

. . . and my mother died the tenth of September that same year . . .

"Good. What else?" He was standing over my shoulder and reading each word I wrote.

. . . my half-sister Fanny was only three and a half at the time and my father raised her from that day as though she were his own daughter. We were cared for first by servants, then by good friends, the Baxters, in Scotland, and finally by his second wife, Claire's mother. But I was the only child of my father's own flesh and his one great love, and we were, from my earliest remembrances, extremely attached.

"There, you have begun," he exclaimed with excitement.

This was the beginning of the story I was to tell. I knew he was right, but I was not the least bit startled, for those airy flights of mine had taken wing from the very moment we first entered Chillon. My days had been filled with them, and my nights made restless by them. I had known for weeks that somewhere in the dark corridors of Chillon, in the shadows in the wind, in the region of my cannibal heart, was buried a story worthy of my lineage, of the mother I never knew save for the printed words she bequeathed me, of the father who pressed me to follow the same road, and for the love that raised me above ordinary talent.

His breath was on my neck; it stirred a careless strand of hair that strayed there and sent a shiver up my back. "It shall be about your father, of course," he said, his voice so close to my ear that I felt its very vibrations in my head, as if I myself had spoken.

I dared not move. His hand was on my arm and I could feel the heat of his palm and the quick, even stroke of his pulse through the sheerness of the cloth of my sleeve.

"*The Maie*," he whispered low. "She is both dark spirit and child of light."

His lips brushed my neck. His gentle hand tucked the wisp of hair that strayed on my bare neck into the bun I wore. I found it hard to breathe. He stepped back and away and I made to rise.

"No, remain as you are. I prefer if your eyes do not meet mine." He had walked back to the fire and sat himself down. "We will sit without words, for we have no need for spoken words this moment. For I have touched you, Mary, and no words of yours could ever dispel that knowledge and none of mine alter the fact."

The dark grew about us. Day had ended and night had lowered and no lamp had yet been lit. The fire dimmed but I was only half conscious of the chill creeping now into the room. Inside my own head I thought I heard that melancholy voice and feeling like a butterfly pinned and on display, I silently begged to be let free. But I was not capable of rising on my own.

"You may wait here if you desire," he said. I turned and saw him standing by the dying flames. "I am going to my chamber until we dine," he added. He walked slowly to the library door. "*The Maie,*" he said, and though I could not see a smile in the shadows of the room, it lurked in his voice and so I knew it was truly there.

I could not remain alone after he had gone. There were only dying embers on the fire and it was as though life had departed and the spirits had not yet accustomed themselves to the *other world*. I therefore returned to Chapuis to wait for Shelley.

The fields were filled with fireflies; they darted between the trees and peopled the land with stars as I walked among them and descended to the lake. I passed a burned-out dock and stood on a safe platform that overlooked the shore. There was a dark boat with a white sail gliding in the distance gently over its surface, and the star-illumined promontories closed in our small cove and there were voices in the wind but I could not hear their words.

19

⌇

While yet a boy I sought for ghosts, and sped
  Through Many a listening chamber, cave and ruin,
  And starlight wood, with fearful steps pursuing
Hopes of high talk with the departed dead.
I called on poisonous names with which our youth is fed;
  I was not heard—I saw them not—
  When musing deeply on the lot
Of life, at that sweet time when winds are wooing
  All vital things that wake to bring
  News of birds and blossoming—
  Sudden, thy shadow fell on me;
I shrieked, and clasped my hands in ecstasy!
          —SHELLEY, "Hymn to Intellectual Beauty,"
                    Switzerland, July, 1816

Shelley had been like a chained spirit for the span of

several days and I was both pleased and relieved that as the day dawned bright and sunny on the morning of his twenty-fourth birthday, we could indulge in some private gaiety, a celebration of our own. Claire and I had travelled into Vevey the previous afternoon and I had purchased a new telescope to replace the lost one and I had made a balloon for Shelley as well. We took the balloon onto the boat to set up but the wind was too strong and so we moved back to the shore, but as soon as the balloon lifted, it burst into flame. For a brief moment it was like a comet above our heads and then it died and only a charred scrap of string remained as testimony to its short but brilliant life.

We did not allow our aerial failure to daunt our spirits, however. I had packed a lunch and with Claire waving to us from our small dock, we set sail upon the lake as though we were departing on an ocean voyage! The wind carried our little boat out without need of our assistance, and so we settled back in each other's arms and Shelley read to me from the Fourth Book of Virgil and I listened. That is, I listened to Shelley's voice, which was like a melody orchestrated by the wind. I could not concentrate on the words of Virgil as fragments of a lost memory kept darting in and out of my mind. A laugh—high, silly, very girlish—and when I closed my eyes, an image would appear. A very pretty young woman, laughing, and as she did, smoothing out the folds of a purple satin gown, a gown of exquisite design, and a shade of purple as luminous and full as ripe wine grapes touched with dew and shining in the sun.

Before we had set out from Chapuis, I had received a letter from Fanny in answer to one of mine, sharing my fears for Harriet, who seemed on the verge of self-destruction, as well as my presentiments for Shelley, who I knew would suffer grievously for it. I had, in mine, added in small comment that I was in many ways quite delivered from torment because I had never set eyes on Harriet or she on me.

You are incorrect, my dear Mary [Fanny wrote], in believing you have never seen Harriet Shelley. If you set your mind back, to a day now nearly four years past (it was the 11th of November, 1812, for I made note of it in my journal), the very day you and Christy Baxter had returned from Scotland. You were, of course, only fifteen and the excitement of your past journey was more enthralling to you than daily life at Skinner Street which you knew to be fraught with comings and goings, and so you and Christy begged leave to share dinner in your chambers where you could exchange confidences. Three guests came to dinner that night—Shelley, Harriet and her sister, Eliza Westbrook, and you did, out of common courtesy, make a brief appearance and greet the dinner guests before disappearing. I recall late that night you commented upon that beautiful lady in the elegant purple satin dress and how attentive her husband had seemed to her. You placed no apparent significance on the meeting so it faded from your memory. But, my dear Mary, that was the evening of your first meeting with Shelley and the one time you did, in true fact, set eyes upon poor Harriet.

:[173]:

It is curious that I had never remembered, nor could not now recall Shelley that night. His name at that time had little meaning to me. Returning as I just had from a year in Scotland, Christy and I had made out that we would do no more than to exchange courtesies with my father's guests so that we would not be detained. I recall nothing of Shelley's face that night though now I remember a slim man's figure beside Harriet, his arm possessively about her exquisitely small waist and *her laugh—high, intoxicated, young*—as his hand found hers as she smoothed her purple gown and, holding it securely, pulled her brazenly even closer to him.

I could not forget that shade of deep, rich purple. Nor the youth and joy in that laugh. It disturbed me mightily and I knew I must cast it out or ruin our day. I closed the book that rested on Shelley's knee and turning to him, raised my face to receive his kiss. His arms were around me, his hands clasped *my* waist now, his lips were warm with our mutual passion and his eyes were filled with love of me.

"Happy birthday, Shelley dear," I whispered. "Happy birthday, my own."

We moored at a deserted length of shore and set immediately to the task of our picnic lunch. Much of the tenseness that I had sensed in Shelley for the last days had taken wing. I did not question its so recent invasion of his body, nor its equally sudden departure. Shelley was a man of rather violent and contrasting moods. Where he remained constant was in his ideals and his loyalties. I suspected much of his uneasiness had to do with a concern over money and the welfare of his children who remained in Harriet's unstable care. Apart from that, he did not think—most especially with Albé's example always before him (Albé had nearly completed the Third Canto of *Childe Harold*)—that he had been fulfilling his commitment as a poet. He had written a very moving poem inspired by the awesomeness of Mont Blanc and was at work on a "Hymn to Intellectual Beauty," but they were apparently fragments of some deeper, more complex philosophical exploring for which he could not as yet find a correct form.

Shelley had explained to me that in "Mont Blanc"— Man is born and dies and his works and ways pass into nothingness, while the Power, of which the giant mountain is both a manifestation and an emblem, dwells apart in its tranquility. Yet, the poem questions, what is mountain and torrent and sky but a desert of death, meaningless and void, if Thought and Love do not inhabit the universe and declare themselves in the brain and heart of man? The poem goes on to say that it is not merely through humanity that this spiritual Power lives, for there is a Presence, or its radiant yet awful shadow, that haunts and startles and waylays us in all that is beautiful, sublime, or heroic. That was Shelley's analysis of the poem's theme and it posed a hard question in my mind—*Is that an atheistic philosophy?* And I answered the question myself—*if that be atheism, it is an atheism us "god-intoxicated" as that of the inspired and excommunicated Spinoza!*

It was this then, his deep-torn conflict on the truth of atheism and his own belief in it, that was disturbing Shelley so greatly, and this questioning he felt driven to answer in his next long work! I knew he felt his atheism had some bearing on Harriet's current instability. I knew he had guilts where this was concerned as well. It was, therefore, not a subject that could be treated calmly. So I spoke of subjects which seemed on safer ground. Now he was bursting with some secret news—a surprise—a plan.

"The world can be ours, Mary," he confided. "What wish would you most want granted?"

"You will think me colourless, indeed," I began, entering into what seemed to be a daydream.

"Come on! Out with it!"

"A cottage—somewhere in the English countryside."

"Done then! I shall write Peacock and enlist his aid as soon as we return to Chapuis." He leant forward and took my chin in his hand. "I received word this morning that a portion of my inheritance is to be released." He was still smiling broadly and the sun was directly overhead and shattered all around him and blinded me so that I fear I had tears in my eyes. He kissed me lightly and then moved to shield me from the glare of the sun. At the same time, it cast a black shadow across his face. "It will be three, perhaps four weeks, before things are settled, the money released and the creditors satisfied. But in any event, it would take that much time for Peacock to find us a suitable house. Mind you, we shall not be rich, but we will be gloriously out of debt."

"Oh, Shelley, how wonderful!"

"You want to return to England then?"

"Of course!"

"We will not be entirely free of problems."

"We can face whatever remains." I felt quite lightened in heart and as I poured us each a glass of local wine from a decanter I had happily brought along, I was conscious of Shelley—sprawled out, his legs extending beyond the blanket we had laid, his long hair disarrayed by the small wind but shining like golden wheat. My heart turned over and I very nearly spilled the wine.

"To our love and our cottage," I said as I handed him his glass.

"To my own Mary," he replied as he emptied the contents.

"Oh," I said, remembering. "Claire."

"She is welcome, and the babe, too."

"You do trust that Albé will act loyally towards Claire and the babe?" I enquired.

"Could you doubt that he would disregard such a moral obligation?"

"I doubt only the true depth of his feeling for Claire."

"He has given no evidence that I can see that he would act other than honourably."

"Considering the evidence that *you* eloped with both Claire and myself, there will be some who might believe you the father," I speculated.

"If so, it will be amusing at least to know we will not return to England with only bored recognition of our return."

I was forced to think now of home, Father and all the problems that would await our return. "Fanny writes Father is in serious debt." It was not a happy subject but the problem of Father was one we would have to face.

"Whatever I can do to help and yet not deny you or my children, I shall do," he assured me.

"I know that, Shelley. And you will always have my gratitude." I turned away. It seemed important Shelley share my true feelings about the only other man in my life, *my father*, and so I pressed on. "He is an imperious and difficult man now, but it was not always so. He has been, through my life, more brother and friend and protector to me than father. And whatever action he has ever taken has always been because he considered it better for my happiness and welfare. Because of his single-sightedness, he has made grievous errors. He should have told Fanny when she was still a child that she was not his true daughter or my true full-sister, but he feared it might cause some disruption between us. He could not see the pain a later telling might engender. Nor the burden my mother's death and his expectations placed upon my capabilities. Nor that his overwhelming love for me could cause me to draw away from him—not because I loved him less, but because I loved you more and his powerful love left no room for any other. But he is, as I do not doubt you will agree, a great man, none-theless, and he has shared a love as controversial and deep-rooted as ours, survived calumny and loss of power, and never has slackened in his contribution to what he believes could benefit mankind. He could say to me or to the world that he disowns me, but it is quite another thing for me to disown him or to accept that he could ever carry those words into action."

I felt better having shared these intimate feelings with Shelley, who, when I turned to him, appeared to be studying me closely. I raised myself up from the ground. "Shall we take a walk along the shore?" I asked.

We walked hand in hand. The wind had slowed and walked in step beside us. The land we trod over was wild, even savage, the soil full of rock that broke through the ground and the grass grew on its own, struggling for existence in tufts between the hard earth. We could have

:[178]:

been on some far uncultivated shore. We walked in silence and in solitude, but our mind's imaginings were as alive as the blue sky and its reflection in the water and, yet, as elusive.

I could not know what forms Shelley's imaginings shaped. For myself, there remained that girlish laugh and a billowing of the richest purple. Returning to England would bring us once again near to Harriet. But now I felt myself to be wholly and inseparably Shelley's one and only and true wife. There was only that blind curtain of deepest purple.

Shelley paused and smiled at me and I answered his smile with my own. I rested my head on his shoulder. It was sharp and hard-edged and Shelley seemed too gaunt. He put his arm about my waist and we turned and walked back to where the remains of our picnic still lay and he helped me pack it all away.

"It was a lovely birthday," he said and handed me a folded piece of paper that had apparently been tucked neatly away in his breast pocket. "My gift to you," he whispered.

I unfolded the paper which was filled with Shelley's evenly slanted and rhythmic hand.

I vowed that I would dedicate my powers
 To thee and thine—have I not kept the vow?
 With beating heart and streaming eyes, even now
I call the phantoms of a thousand hours
Each from his voiceless grave: they have in visioned
  bowers
 Of studious zeal or love's delight
 Outwatched with me the envious night—

Haunted Summer

They know that never joy illumned my brow
   Unlinked with hope that thou wouldst free
   This world from its dark slavery,
   That thou—O awful LOVELINESS,
Wouldst give whate'er these words cannot express.

The day becomes more solemn and serene
   When noon is past—there is a harmony
   In autumn, and a lustre in its sky,
Which through the summer is not heard or seen,
As if it could not be, as if it had not been!
   Thus let thy power, which like the truth
   Of nature on my passive youth
Descended, to my onward life supply
   Its calm—to one who worships thee,
   And every form containing thee,
   Whom, SPIRIT fair, thy spells did bind
To fear himself, and love all human kind.

Shelley had completed his "Hymn to Intellectual
Beauty" and in giving me these last two stanzas, said
more than spoken words could say—saying I held the
power of intellectual beauty as he did himself and pro-
mising us both a peace in the autumn soon to come
which would dispel the restless stirrings of this haunted
summer.

20

Polidori was served a writ of *arrêt* for having *"casse ses lunettes et fait tomber son chapeau"* of the apothecary who he claimed sold him bad magnesia. He explained to us that he found it bad by experiment of sulphuric acid colouring it a red-rose and that the magnesia was chiefly alumina, as proved by succenate and carbonate of ammonia. Still, there was the writ of *arrêt* and Polidori, with Shelley, myself and an advocate Albé had employed, rode into Geneva for Polidori's court appearance.

He was brought to trial before five judges, the apothecary having accused him of calumny. The little man sat rather fearfully across the full length of the courtroom and Polidori laughed openly at him as he strode towards the box. There was a great deal of confusion as Polidori turned to the judges and told them he would not allow the advocate to plead his case and that he would, with the court's permission, plead for himself. Finally, permission was granted.

His *performance* was most convincing. One wondered if Polidori had not missed his calling and should have apprenticed to Kean! That he had seen the great actor perform seemed likely, for as he spoke and in the use of his hands, the image of Kean in the one theatrical I had the good fortune to see him in, came immediately to my mind! The judges were instantly won over and all five, as if one, turned a disapproving eye on the poor apothecary, who lost his case. Though, with some remaining justice, Polidori was made to pay twelve florins for the spectacles and costs.

One would have thought then that Polidori would have been filled with triumph, gloating, even more arrogant than usual. But during the coach ride back to Diodati he was sunk in gloom, as if he had so thoroughly convinced himself that his appearance in court was, indeed, a performance, that he was suffering from post-performance melancholy, a complaint I had often heard among theatre people. However, I hastily dismissed this theory when I recalled Polidori's state after his physical fight with Albé in Chillon, for he was reacting the same way now. He was suffering, I decided, from bouts of depression. And then, thinking back to all his discussions on drugs and poisons (he was forever speaking of prussic acid, and oil of amber, and blowing into veins and suffocating by charcoal) and the several times I had heard him flippantly, yet with some conviction, speak of suicide, I was most painfully concerned. And recalling that after Albé had discovered him in the act of reading and copying his journal, he had actually written Albé a suicide note claiming he planned to kill himself, my anxiety increased. Albé had joked about it and none of us had really taken it seriously, for Polidori was inclined towards melodramatics and he was a practising Catholic who must regard suicide as a mortal sin. But now, as I sat beside him in the coach and studied his profile reflected in the window as he stared out and away into the far distance, presentiments stirred within me. Polidori could easily be tripping over the tender line of madness, and I was certain he was already deeply in the grip of melancholia.

When we arrived at Diodati there was a great fire blazing in the library hearth. And as the day, though not too great a summer failure, was nonetheless chill and turning colder as it neared evening, we gladly drew close to its warmth. Claire was seated at the desk in the dimming light copying for Albé, who rose to greet us but never inquired the outcome of the trial. Polidori went directly to his room but returned a short time later with his stringed musical instrument and, seating himself in a far corner and apart, strummed a melancholy strain to and for himself.

Albé was overjoyed to see Shelley. He was in very good humour and he and Shelley exchanged some light-hearted comments on local gossip. He was pacing back and forth across the room all the while and finally came to a stop beside Claire.

"Have you finished copying the poem?" he inquired.

"Yes, but it is not yet dry," Claire replied as she dusted the paper she had been working on.

Albé took it from her hand. "There may be errors," Claire added. "It is most difficult to concentrate in the midst of so much confusion."

I had taken a seat beside the hearth and was writing in my journal, which I had brought along with me.

"Mary seems to have no problem." Albé smiled and came closer to me, leaning towards me. "Cool, calm, collected Mary. Working on your ghost story?"

"No, I am making an entry in my journal."

"Ah, hear that, Poli? Mary has a journal as well. You might make note of that to Murray."

Polidori struck a dissonant chord in reply as Albé, never turning his head in Polidori's direction, crossed over to Shelley and presented him with the sheet of paper he had taken from Claire.

"Tell me what you think of it," he asked Shelley.

He stood over Shelley for a few moments as Shelley set to reading it, then he nervously strode away and to the table, where a tray of drinks had been set and poured himself a full glass of claret. He was watching Shelley closely. Polidori began a new piece and Albé turned on him. "Will you stop playing that infernal instrument!" he snapped. There was immediate silence in the room. As difficult as it was, I raised my eyes to Polidori's face. It was blank of expression, a child's chalkboard wiped clean. Shelley lowered the poem and straightened in his chair and Albé was instantly at his side.

"Well? How do you like it?"

"Least of anything I ever read of yours," Shelley told him forthrightly. "A bad imitation I would say of Faust, and, in addition, there are two entire lines from Southey's *The Curse of Kehama*."

Shelley leant forward again, planning to read the plagiarized lines aloud, but before he could do so, Albé swept the paper from his hands, crushed it in his palms and then tossed it most accurately into the heart of flames.

"All writers are plagiarists," he said with a dry laugh. "It is a bad thing to have too good a memory." He leant against the mantle and watched intently as the paper flared into flame and then disintegrated into ash. "I do believe there is as great a joy in burning a poem as in publishing one."

Claire sighed so deeply we all turned to her. "Thank heaven I have the original!" she exclaimed.

I contained myself with great difficulty, but Shelley laughed. "You may thank heaven, Claire, but some credit I believe must be granted his Lordship!"

There was an awkward moment and then Albé laughed. He was the small boy now, aware that Shelley knew all the while that his dramatic gesture of burning the poem was exactly that, *only a gesture.* He drew a chair close to Shelley and the two of them began an earnest discussion. Their voices grew soft and intimate, punctuated by the crackle of the fire. Claire tiptoed across the room and asked me in a whisper if I would care to take a walk, but it was growing dark and the day's excursion had tired me. She sat down on the floor at my feet and leaning against the leg of the chair, her own legs clasped tightly to her chest, listened closely so that she could hear all the two men said.

"Is it madness," Shelley was saying, "to look forward to a time when a new golden age will return to earth, when all the different creeds and systems of the world

:[185]:

will be amalgamated into one, when man will be free from shackles, civil and religious?"

"Perhaps not madness—but of a certain, dangerous!" Albé replied.

I had turned once again to watching Polidori. Holding his instrument to him, he crossed to the window, seeming to merge at once with the shadows of night.

"Who would not rather be born two or three centuries hence, eh Shelley?" Albé was saying. "I suppose we shall soon be travelling by air vessels and at length find our way to the moon, in spite of the want of atmosphere." He leant back in his chair. "Do you imagine, that in former stages of this planet, wiser creatures than ourselves did not exist? All our boasted inventions, Shelley, are but shadows of what has been—the dim images of the past. Who knows whether, when a comet shall approach the globe to destroy it, men will not tear rocks from their foundations by means of steam and hurl mountains against the flaming mass? Then, Shelley, *then* there shall be the inevitable war . . . *the war with heaven.*"

Polidori turned away from the window and walked behind Albé and Shelley towards the door. His eyes were vacant, bare windows of a deserted house. As he passed by me, a folded piece of paper fell from his hand to the floor. Careful not to disturb Claire, who rested against the opposite side of my chair, I cautiously leant over to retrieve it. I spread the paper out on my lap. What was written on it was in Albé's easily recognizable handwriting. A ragged edge suggested it had been torn from a book or journal.

"Were Death an evil, would I let thee live?"

I folded the paper as quietly as I could and slipped it

inside the sleeve of my dress. I felt at that moment like a conspirator of Polidori's, but in my heart I knew anything else—attention called, the paper shown, would have been an indication of betrayal and Polidori was in a state of depression that could not at this time endure that weight.

21

For my own part, I had never seen a ghost except once in a dream. I feared it in my sleep; I awoke trembling, and lights and the speech of others could hardly dissipate my fear. But this day, I travelled to Chillon on my own, and believed I saw a ghost for the second time in my life.

Shelley had confided to me that *his* ghost story was to be theatrical, a drama that he would direct and in which we four, untutored in our lines beforehand, would be the principal players. It was my suggestion that I journey to Chillon alone that same afternoon to speak to Ianthe and in a sense to take her into our confidence and attempt to diminish her antagonism.

I departed Chapuis by coach while the sun was still high and arrived at Chillon not long before twilight. The gateman bid me enter but the castle appeared deserted. I went immediately to Ianthe's quarters, but there was no reply to my insistent knocking. I decided I should look within the castle for her and entered an open rear door. A tremendous sense of loneliness at once seized me, and as I walked through the vast halls and spacious apartments calling Ianthe by name, I thought I heard the chimes of the Ave Maria on the chapel bell. I stood by a window where I could see, but the bell hung motionless in the open belfry.

The far mountains had lost their sunset tinge; no wind ruffled the shimmering face of the lake. I was conscious as I continued to walk through the vacant chambers that none save I awakened the echoes of those stone floors.

I left the castle and stood in the courtyard. From where I stood I could see that the guard had left his post for the day and only my own coachman stood by the gate. It seemed to me likely that Ianthe would be in the dungeons or in the rooms beyond and I descended the stairway without qualm or fear.

I entered its Gothic interior somehow filled with sensations of the most poignant grief, and as I stood alone and glanced the length of the dungeons, there was, I thought, a *sigh*. Of course, it could have been the wind, but I doubted not that moment that it was the Prisoner of Chillon. He had once been here, caged by these dank walls, his breath had mingled with this same atmosphere, his step had been on these same stones. The wind rose and I thought I heard—I felt—I know not what—but I trembled. And I knelt upon the stones and trembled more, awe-struck and afraid. And as my glance moved once more along the row of pillars a chain appeared to lift itself as though pulled forward by a straining man. It was *his* pillar, *his* chain, a loose stone shifted where *his* foot might have pressured, and, in the dim path of fleeting light that passed the pillar's way, I thought a shadow stept from the restless shade.

I got up from my knees and walked in its direction. The fear had left me. I trembled no more. But as I neared his pillar, the chain fell back in place. I paused and as I did all was gone and the dungeons were once more a silent, darkening tomb.

To my great astonishment I finally came upon Ianthe standing before the altar in the little chapel. I had caught her unawares, and as early evening had enveloped the castle, she appeared to loom up out of the darkness like the topmast on a deserted ship in black, uncharted waters. I knew it was she, even as she stood, all night and shadow, but she was startled by my intrusion, and though I said clearly, *Madame Shelley, Ianthe*, she nonethless arched her back like a cat facing danger, and lighting a candle which she then held before her, she called out, "Who approaches?"

"Madame Shelley," I repeated and heard the echo of my footsteps as I drew closer.

Her face was yellow in the flame's reflection, her eyes two ashen coals. "What do you want?" she demanded.

"I came to speak with you."

"The castle is locked. Visiting hours past. No one has notified me of your coming."

"I have spent an hour's time in search of you."

She stood without any reaction. "News is on the way that his Lordship and his friends will be here at midnight," I continued. "I am glad I have preceded it, as I wished to speak with you first."

She lowered the candle so that I could no longer see
her face clearly, and to further distort, the candle's
smoke crept serpentlike between us. "His Lordship and
his friends," the voice parted the smoke, making dozens
of writhing reptiles of it, "are hell-bound savages who
respect no gods and who talk with the Devil among
them." She raised the candle now and brought it so close
to my face that I felt the heat of its flames dangerously
near me. "And if the Devil has not yet overcome you,
Madame, you would desert such company, or—" she
paused and eased her hold on the candle. I could see a
faint and wistful smile on her face and observed for the
first time the quantity of tired years that rested upon the
heavy support of her broad, sharp bones. "Or," she
repeated, "destroy the Devil in your midst."

"You are under a misconception, and it is that that I
have come to speak to you about. His Lordship is a poet,
one of England's greatest, and my husband, Mr. Shelley,
son of Sir Timothy Shelley, grandson to Sir Bysshe
Shelley, is a great poet as well. I grant you our nocturnal
visits seem suspect of heathenish designs, but in fact they
are intended in good spirit and are in the best tradition
of the search for truth and art. We merely exchange
stories, each one of us taking his turn on a particular
night. But because the story-tellers are endowed with the
ability to make their tales at once real to us all, we do, I
fear, in our stunned responses appear as though Devil-
sent."

She had been silent and seemed to listen attentively,
and so I dared to step a little closer and at the same time
present her with the two small volumes I had brought

with me (one of Shelley's early romances and one containing a French translation of the first two cantos of Lord Byron's *Childe Harold*). "Please take these small gifts," I said. "They are but a token and I apologize that the one, my husband's, is in English and therefore more difficult for you to read. But perhaps you will still enjoy what you may understand, for I assure you both volumes are wrought by man's hand and not the Devil's!"

I thought for a moment that she would refuse the offering, but she did reach out and take the volumes from me, though her expression never varied and she remained austerely silent.

"My husband perceives you might be Greek by birth and though his spoken French is, I fear, a bit wanting, he is fluent in Greek and could, if you so desired, or found need, translate some portions of his book into that beautiful language for you."

She still made no response and I shifted uneasily, for the stones had grown cold beneath the fragile soles of the slippers I had foolishly worn. "There is one thing more," I added. "I am in a sense the spokesman for my companions and want to beg your forbearance of any inconveniences we have caused you. We shall visit Chillon only once or twice more before summer's end sees our departure." It seemed she had decided to remain silent. "I will take my leave then," I said and turned to go.

"Madame . . ."

"Yes?" I faced her once more. There was sadness in her eyes and her skin appeared as yellowed as pages in a musty book.

"Once I was as beautiful as you," she whispered. And

then with her bare fingers she extinguished the flame of the candle and save for the shadow of smoke, we were both in pitchy blackness.

I could smell the melting wax and something else—the damp that clung to aged stone and the dust of air entombed.

"We trust we do not disturb you later this night," I said and then, as quickly as was possible without seeming to flee, I walked back across the chapel and started out the door. She had not moved to follow and somehow I felt a great sense of relief. I turned back for one moment. *"Au revoir,"* I said.

But there was only the obscure dark and in it I could no longer define even the dead candle's smoky shadow.

The air was raw and presaged rain before morning. I drew my shawl tightly about my shoulders and made my way to the gate. A riderless horse neighed loudly at my approach and as I made to open the gate a figure sprang from the rear seat of my coach and opened the gate door for me.

"Your Lordship!" I said surprised.

"What the bloody hell were you doing here alone?" he shouted.

"Come to speak with Ianthe," I replied. We stood before the gate, Chillon a dark prehistoric mammoth behind us, *he* blocking my advance towards the warmth and protection of the coach.

"Women are totally irrational," he snapped angrily. "That Greek dragoness is mad and quite capable of setting the entire castle in flames and you with it!"

"I doubt that. Ianthe is tortured but I do not think mad."

"What do you know of madness?" he asked without expecting me to reply, for he took me by the arm and led me aside. "We shall walk for a bit. My legs are stiff from riding."

As I knew he often liked to take such long rides by himself, I did not question his *own* irrationality. Albé was an expert horseman. He was, for that matter, a superior sportsman in all respects.

We walked along the side of the road and the coach and the horse followed a discreet distance behind. He did not seem to mind the chill or to notice that I was not dressed for a walk on such an evening. He strode just a pace before me so that I had to run a bit to keep up.

"I cannot walk so swiftly," I finally said breathlessly.

He slowed his pace and measured his limping step to mine.

"Shall I not talk?" I asked.

"Shall Mont Blanc disappear?" he replied. Then he took my hand and drew me down a path, away from the road and towards the lake shore. "Wait there," he called to the coachman. In a moment we were at the foot of a small rise to the road and the coach lost from our sight.

The moon lighted our path. We were walking in the direction of the monkey's funeral pyre and stayed silent until we stood beside it—a few charred stones remaining only to mark it.

"What is it, Albé, that makes you demand so much of love that even death seems a betrayal?" I asked softly.

For an instant I thought he had not heard me. Then he glanced up from his intense study of the earth beneath his feet and locked his gaze with mine. Terror coursed through me and I felt my heart constrict. He raised his hand and touched my cheek—my brow. I could feel his pulse throb in his finger ends. I dared not move. I felt paralyzed—and yet never quite so unquieted within. I tried to step aside, to walk as swiftly as I was able back to the road. But for that moment I was Albé's hypnotized prisoner and my body my own gaol.

"Death is the great betrayal," he said and his voice seemed curiously harsh. "The only one that matters."

Self-betrayal is greater! I wanted to scream, but I was speechless. His hand caught my chin and held it, tilting it so that my face was raised to him, for we stood on uneven ground and he was, for the first time, a full head taller than I. The gesture was not gentle, spoke of a controlled, yet recognizable violence.

"You think Shelley incapable of betrayal," he said, "but Shelley is only man, after all, and shall perish like the rest. And he is not as hardy as you, Mary." A smile flickered in his eyes, then died. "You are the strongest woman I have ever known. You shall outlive us all, I am certain. Then you will understand that even Shelley is capable of betrayal."

His hand slid down my neck, my shoulder, my arm. He drew me close to him. I still could not draw away. His body was hard and solid, and the cloth of his jacket rough-textured.

"Shelley's world is a romantic world," he whispered. "Is that where his great appeal rests? Is it his sensitivity that makes him so irresistible?" He held me now with both hands. Their strength shocked me and I was aware that even if my will should return to me, removing myself from his grasp would be no easy matter.

"And yet," he said, his face now large and near my own, his breath upon my dry lips, "some say it is the Devil in me that makes *me* so irresistible."

He crushed his lips to mine. It was, at first, a wounding gesture, a blow, and then *oh, who could speak other than of the flesh being capable of the greatest betrayal!—* movement returned to me and I felt a helpless rushing towards him.

It was he who drew away first. There was a large stone near us and I lowered myself to it, unable to remain standing another moment and he came and sat beside me. He did not touch me and I was grateful for that small kindness.

"You are an astonishing woman, Mary," he ventured at last, "and perhaps, after all, you will be the first of your sex to prove equality with nobler men. But can you bear that pain? For surely it will prove to be a heavy burden."

"Women have endured pain since the beginning. You might say we have been born to it."

"We are monsters, the pair of us, for the greatest aberration man can have is to hold with ideas not accepted whilst he lives." He sighed deeply. "Shelley, of course, is another matter. His speculations are mystical, his supposed feelings illusions, his creations are of another world which he alone inhabits."

The mention of my own dear Shelley's name at this time caused a stab of remorse to chill my heart. The wind had risen and my hair blew across my face, but I held my

:[197]:

arms to myself, tightly gripping my shawl, for I was shivering and could feel the cold deep within me.

He stared at me with some surprise. "Guilt?" he asked sharply, and then when I could not reply, began to laugh. "You are no truer to your philosophy than your mother before you. But in spite of it, I find you damned exciting. We are truly a match, Mary. You know that, and I know that, and I will confide a small secret to you, *Shelley knows it as well.* And we shall never be done with each other, even, Mary, when death do us part."

He removed his jacket then and placed it around my shoulders and, after doing so, brushed back the hair from my face, a casual gesture, really, but there was a depth of emotion in his eyes that frightened me.

"We will return to the coach," he said. "You are chilled through." But he made no gesture to move from the spot. "Could you love me as deeply as you love Shelley?" he asked at last.

"As I told you once before, Milord, I am quite sure I could never love anyone as I love Shelley," I replied quietly but without hesitation.

"But you find me irresistible?" he grinned.

"I find you—human—and myself more so than I deemed possible."

He studied me for a moment and then, glancing away, walked past me and started up the short incline to the coach.

"Are you certain you can do without your jacket?" I called after him.

"The only thing I cannot do without," he replied over his shoulder, as I followed him, "is memory. Unless it be

the knowledge that all humankind shares the same in-
constant heart."

We were over the rise and soon tucked warmly beneath
a travelling robe inside the coach. I had returned his
jacket, but though it was damp and chill, he threw it
down on the seat.

"You are a woman before your time and I sometimes
think I am a man after my own," he said slowly and after
a great deal of thought, as soon as we were settled in the
coach. His eyes burned deeply into my own. Then he
turned and stared out into the darkness, though nothing
could be seen, and sat unspeaking and never glancing my
way for the full time the drive back to our respective
homes required.

It was the most painful journey I had ever taken. No
amount of concentration could exorcise the emotion I
had felt for this man. His presence filled every cavity of
space in the coach and I felt as though I might choke, so
stifling was it. His silence made it grow denser and my
inability to break that silence only intensified it. I feared
a seizure might well grip my heart and I would never
return to my Shelley's side. At last the coach turned off
the road and drew up before Chapuis.

"Shall we meet at Diodati?" I was able to inquire as I
stept down from the coach, so released did I feel by this
gesture! He had not disembarked with me but remained
seated well back in the darkness, so that when he replied,
his answer came as though disembodied.

"I am continuing on to see the Governor and will call
for you and Shelley and Claire on my return."

"The Governor?"

"I have asked him to relieve Ianthe of her duties at Chillon. But I am distressed to find her still there and will ask him to order her immediate removal."

I stept in as close as I could to the door of the coach. He had stretched extravagantly across the interior, his legs flung across it, but his face was shadowed and hidden from my view.

"Please, your Lordship, Albé, *I beg you*—do not."

"She is mad, possessed."

"Perhaps, but Chillon is her *life*—and in a matter of short weeks it will have no part of yours, for I know you speak of Italy and the sun awaiting you there."

"I will return in two or three hours," he said, dismissing my request without further consideration. He signalled the coachman, who was instantly at my side, guiding me away and to the door of Chapuis. I flung it open and ran to the privacy of my room.

I was not sure if it was the cruelty, the coldness he was displaying towards Ianthe, or the tremulous warmth he once again excited in me. But I was aware that no other person's voice had ever had the same power of awakening melancholy in me as his. And, whereas I could listen timelessly to the tête-à-têtes between him and Shelley at Diodati, I could not talk with him alone without suffering tormenting unease, for when he spoke and Shelley was not there to answer, it was as the thunder without rain—the form of the sun without heat or light.

I could not understand why he, by his mere presence and voice, had the power of exciting such deep and shifting emotions within me, but I was resolved from that night forth never to spend a moment alone in his company.

22

When Shelley came to tell me several hours later that the coach had arrived to convey us to Chillon, I was dry-eyed and seemed freshly woke from sleep. I hurried to dress and supped lightly from a tray in my room and was soon seated between Shelley and Claire facing Lord Byron and Polidori in the coach. Claire sat huddled and sleepy in her corner, a child up past her bedtime. And Polidori, from the glassiness of his stare and his detachment appeared to be drugged once again. Shelley and Albé were in high spirits and were engaged in energetic conversation for the length of the journey. For the first time, whilst side by side with Shelley, I felt alone. Oh, how alone, Shelley could not have suspected, or he would have turned from Albé to embrace me.

There were no lights in the castle to greet us and Ianthe, if there at all, was either asleep in her darkened quarters or silent to our coming. We went directly to the dungeons and Shelley immediately took the night's entertainment into his hands.

"This night we will not be joined in a circle or be seated before the Prisoner's Pillar." He took my hand and the others followed and he led us past all the pillars to the very rear of the dungeons where on a dais of uneven stone stood *The Gallows*.

We stood at the foot facing Shelley, who had climbed onto the dais. "My ghost story is in a manner of speaking a theatrical but, if successful, shall be a new and perhaps perilous journey into the unknown, the occult, the world of mysticism, the experience of transcendentalism. And you, my friends, shall be my players and thereupon your own sorcerers, exorcising your own ghosts.

"It will be played out in this fashion: Each of you in turn shall kneel beneath the gallows, while below shall be your court of last appeal of which I will try to be a silent member. But one member at a time shall become your grand inquisitor." He smiled easily. "You may be asking yourself, *What then does he, the creator, do?* And I answer, *The same as all author-creators; appoint my characters, for after that their actions, their lives truly take hold and you but hold the quill whilst they draw blood from the point and etch their own veiny words.* We shall, as well, perform in a darkened theatre, this dais our black stage, for we are travelling inward, to the midnight of the mind and the depths of hidden soul. Shall there be a volunteer to begin Act One?"

"Without question it shall be I!" Albé declared and hoisted himself up onto the dais alongside Shelley.

I had not known what Shelley's play should be, but

now as he glanced at me and our eyes met, I understood that this macabre game had been conceived with the intention of exorcising my fears so as to make a mockery of them and grind them to phantom dust. If I could have halted Shelley then—*but* it was not possible. For I was spellbound.

Shelley put out his candle. Then Claire reached out and extinguished her own. I blew mine out. The last was Polidori who stood beside Claire, more in a state of detached apathy now than stupor, for the ride, the night, the chill appeared to waken some response in him, even if that response be apathy! Shelley then came down and stood beside me.

Albé was on the dais by himself. His candle still flickered and the ancient gallows' beam above his head caught licks of light on its gnarled surface. The smile of assurance had faded from his pale face, his bravado gone. He was that moment in quandary. A moment later his candle light was snuffed out and only its vapourish trail could be distinguished in the dark. It moved downward and to the stone floor of the dais and then was gone. Albé had kneeled but could not do so before us whilst any glimmer of light yet remained.

There was a long numbing silence.

"What are you thinking?" Shelley asked Albé, though his voice sounded strange and hollow and unfamiliar to my ear.

It was a long moment before Albé's reply. "A curious thing, an odd circumstance—that my daughter Ada, my wife Annabelle, my half-sister Augusta, my natural daughter Medora, my mother, my sister's mother, and myself are or were all only children. My sister's mother

:[203]:

had only my half-sister by that second marriage and my father had only me by his second marriage with my mother. For some reason it has just come to my mind that such a complication of only children, all tending to one family, is singular enough, and looks like fatality almost. But then, I am also thinking that the fiercest animals—the lions and tigers—have the rarest numbers in their litters."

He grew silent and for a short time I thought he might not speak again. Claire shifted nervously on the ground beside me. When Albé spoke next it was as though to an empty chamber for he had lost awareness of our presence.

"I have also been thinking lately a good deal of Mary Duff and how very odd that I should have been so utterly fond of that girl at an age when I could neither feel passion nor know the meaning of the word. My mother used always to rally me about this childish amour and years later, I was sixteen and . . . ."

He paused in mid-sentence as though another memory had intruded upon his continuity of thought. Then he sighed deeply and at last continued, his voice vague in memory, softer.

"Mary Duff . . . yes . . . My mother told me one day, 'Oh, Byron, I have had a letter from Edinburgh, from Miss Abercromby and your old sweetheart, Mary Duff, is married to a Mr. Coe.' I really cannot explain or account for my feelings at that moment, but they nearly threw me into convulsions and alarmed my mother so much that after I grew better, she generally avoided the subject with me—though she discussed it endlessly with all her acquaintances. But I recollect all we said to each other then—Mary Duff and I—all our caresses, her features, my restlessness, my torment. I certainly had no sexual ideas for years afterwards—for I was then not eight years old—yet my love for that girl was so violent that her marriage eight years later was like a thunderstroke—it nearly choked me . . . . *Mary Duff . . . Mary Duff . . .* " he whispered. And then so softly, I was not sure I had heard accurately, "Clare . . . . " I felt Claire's hand lightly touch mine. "Clare," he repeated and then began to speak more confidently.

"My school friendships were with me passions, for I was always violent, but only one has endured until now. I was sixteen and he was younger—and through the years that followed, I never could hear the name Clare without a beating of the heart, even now, for that was his name. Curious I have but seen him once since—and that was only this past spring as I was set to leave England and he had just returned.

"He was lean and golden and had changed so little . . . . " He took a deep breath and it trembled within him. "Our meeting annihilated for a moment all the years between the present time and the days at Harrow. It was a new and inexplicable feeling, like rising from the grave, to me. Clare, too, was much agitated—more it seemed, than even myself, for I could feel his heart beat to his finger's end—unless—unless, it was the pulse of my own which made me think so."

"Were you not the cause of his shame and expulsion from school?" Polidori interrupted, a cold steel edge to his voice.

"It was I who was sent down. He—knew no *shame.*"

"He told you that? *Clare* told you that?" Polidori sneered from the obscurity of the dark.

"It is singular how soon we lose the impression of what ceases to be constantly before us. There is little distinct left without an effort of memory—then indeed the lights are rekindled for a moment—*He knew no shame.*"

"Can you be sure that imagination is not the torch bearer?" Polidori pressed.

"I can be sure," Albé—*the witness*—answered angrily, then was silent.

"Continue," Shelley urged gently.

"My hopeless attachment to *Clare* threw me out alone on a wide, wide sea. I recollect then meeting my sister Augusta at General Harcourt's in Portland Place that same year. She claims I had altered into manhood and truth, though I was not sensible of the change, I could account for its happening and believe in its existence, for Augusta now appeared to me a woman, and a woman who might have been the mirror image of myself."

"Yourself," Claire interrupted and her venom made splinters of the dark, "always yourself."

"Guilty! Guilty!" Polidori shouted, all signs of his apathy now gone.

I felt Claire rise beside me and felt the stiffness of her skirt against my cheek as she leant forward towards the dais.

"You alone must reign," she spat at him, "be feared, be thought of, all others are to be sacrificed, living victims at the shrine of your self-love. What have you done to merit so much devotion? Ask your heart, if it be

:[206]:

not turned to stone—ask it what you have done. *What have you done?"*

"Guilty! Guilty!" Polidori shrieked and then jumped up to the dais and though in that darkness I could not truly see him, I was aware of his sharp body cutting through the heaviness and was mesmerized by the erratic beat of foot on stone as he danced a madman's dance around the edge of the dais, the sound seeming like a frightened man's heartbeat magnified a million times. God only knew why he did not fall as he continued to dance, screaming all the while, "Guilty! Guilty!"

"I demand my child! By what right do you rob me of my child?" Claire shouted.

By a coincidence of time Shelley struck a light and Albé raised himself from his knees, and as he did, the gallows' noose uncoiled itself and fell limply just above his head. Claire screamed and Polidori, who was still dancing about as one possessed, stopped suddenly in his tracks and in a moment his face was once again blank and unresponsive, and his body a bellows emptied of breath.

Albé stood impassively, not moving. Shelley started towards him, anticipating he might faint. But a slow smile spread across Albé's face and then he rocked with laughter and jumped down from the dais and threw his arms around Shelley's shoulders.

"Not even Kean could follow that act!" he roared and directed Shelley out of the dungeons.

Claire looked as though she might be reduced to tears and raised her arm to cover her face like some small and injured sparrow. I took her by the waist and turned her round and guided her step to follow Albé and Shelley.

:[207]:

"Shall his Lordship always be permitted to speak the last word?" Polidori called after us.

We all turned back. Polidori stood holding the noose in his hands, toying with it.

I glanced at Shelley. He did not move. But then Albé stept forward and walked by himself to the foot of the dais.

"By God, you do look the part of an executioner, Poli!" he laughed harshly.

"To kill or not to kill, that is the question," Polidori replied sharply.

"Are you asking that question, Poli?" Albé enquired.

"With me it remains a question, Milord. For you it is a *fait accompli*."

"Are you saying I am guilty of murder?"

"Ah, guilt! That is a separate issue! If I should place this noose about my neck and hang myself, would I be guilty of murder? Or would the forces leading to my murder bear the guilt?"

"You could simply walk away from those *forces*, Poli. As simply as I can walk away from you this moment." And Albé turned and limped towards the exit.

Polidori in one swift movement slipped the noose over his own head. Shelley and I immediately started towards him.

"Milord!" Polidori shouted.

Albé did not slacken his step.

"Milord!" Polidori screamed and then he made to tighten the noose.

Shelley and I were now beside him and between us restrained him and managed to remove the rope from about his neck. Though he fought us, he seemed lacking his usual strength and in a few moments, Shelley had him by one arm and I the other.

"Let me stand alone," he commanded.

We exchanged worried glances but did as he asked. He took one unsteady step forward and paused. Albé had already left the dungeons and Claire had followed him. The three of us were alone.

"An execution without an audience is hardly an execution at all," Polidori said and then walked swiftly before us, never once glancing back or acknowledging our presence.

23

I spent hours alone now in solitary walks. Something very strange and frightening and filled with wonder was happening to me. I cannot explain except to say that for the first time Shelley had a rival to fear. But it was not as one might suppose, for it was the woman inside me whom Shelley had never met and who was constantly at work wooing me from Shelley or from any other man who threatened total possession—and, thus, her extinction. I was fighting for my life and yet at the same time, for Shelley and my life together, but they were separate and it seemed most important to me that he understood. I prayed he would. For I was a woman in labour and that must be a time without men and so I had been walking by the shore and through the vineyards and on the path where the berries grew which led to the small mountain behind Chapuis.

My story was beginning to take form. The very night of Shelley's *theatrical* marked its first throb of life. It was entirely too premature for me yet to know what shape it might inhabit or what voice it would ascribe to use, but its growing presence became more evident each day. And torn between my loyalty to its development and Shelley's needs, I found to my bewilderment that it was this un-born fetus of creativity within me to whom I had become aligned.

Mention had been made that we would not go again to Chillon, and Albé had given up asking me if I had my story. A disenchantment of the entire venture had set in, and I was only too happy to conclude that our nocturnal visits to Chillon had drawn to a close. But this child within me was a thing apart and it was much too late and dangerous to abort it now.

I began to think about things that had never before occurred to me. It surprised me to recognize for the first time that Shelley and my father were much the same sort of men and that my relations with each had been equally consuming and that for one part of my life I had wanted to be most what my father desired me to be, and that in the other part of my life—*the now*—I was striving to be what Shelley desired most for me to be. And I wondered at that.

Strangers to us might not see the relationship of Shelley to my father, but they were both dedicated, brilliant and talented men, of strong convictions. Each required constant attendance *and more*, an immediate audience, a devoted disciple but one they felt equal to the task.

No tutor ever demanded as much from a student as my

father had, or contributed as greatly to her education. At fifteen, I was certain there could not be much more to learn and then I met Shelley and each day we would read together and study Greek and other languages and history and philosophy and the work of great writers. And in the questioning and searching turn it gave my thoughts, there was seldom time for wild reverie. But since that night of Shelley's theatrical a week past, Claire had not spent much time at Diodati and Polidori journeyed into Geneva nearly every day and remained until half the night was gone. And so Albé had been quite deserted, save for Shelley, which meant, they were spending more time together and I had much opportunity to be alone.

Day was fading and the mountains were receding in the distance. I stood on a small rise and Chapuis took on twilight colours beneath me. The sky was streaked with violet and the sun a searing rim behind the far mountain, and Shelley stood in purple shadow, his features undistinguishable, and about the entire scene, a sense of unreality. Shelley had not seen me yet, he stood beside Albé and they were lost in conversation. Albé saw me first and he waved and then Shelley turned. I must have appeared an alien shadow only among the small firs of the hillside, but he called:

"Mary, come join us!"

Let me love the trees, Shelley, the skies, and the ocean. Let me, in my fellow creature, love that which is, let me love and admire neither adorning nor diminishing that which I love, and above all—Oh, Shelley—listen—

:[213]:

listen—*Above all, let me fearlessly descend into the remotest corners of my own mind and dislodge any evil spirit hidden there!*

They waited for me on the pathway and we entered the cottage together. Claire was in the sitting room. A fire burned in the hearth and a proper tea tray was set out and waiting. She sat quietly over her needlework in a corner, and for the first time I perceived the gentle rise where the babe nestled. She did not glance up as we entered but concentrated wholly upon her handwork. "Oh, Mary, there is tea and madeleines," she said demurely and then her lips moved silently as she counted off her stitches.

I poured a round of tea and we sat drinking it stiffly.

"Albé has suggested we might go into Geneva tonight and see the inside of a gaming house," Shelley mentioned.

"I have always found gamblers unhappy people and the prospect of seeing them in the grip of their obsession does not please me. I think not," I said, "not I, at least. Go most certainly if you wish."

"Oh, I have a notion gamblers are as happy as most people, being always excited," Albé commented. "Every turn of the card, and cast of the dice, keeps the gambler alive. Besides one can game ten times longer than one can do anything else!" He laughed and Shelley with him. "I hate card games but I rather love the rattle and dash of the box and dice, and the glorious uncertainty, not only of good luck or bad luck, but of any luck at all." He smiled to himself. "I have thrown as many as fourteen mains running and carried off all the cash on the table occasionally, but the money never mattered to any consequence—it is the *delight* of the thing that pleases me."

"Is that where old Poli takes himself? Into the gaming houses in Geneva?" Claire called across the room. "I would think he might have found an opium den as well."

"You can be such a damned bitch, Claire," Albē snapped.

Claire glanced over to Shelley, expecting him to defend her.

"I really think something should be done about Polidori," I interrupted.

"What in heaven can be done?" Albē said archly. "He is a grown man."

"He is losing reason. I am certain of it. In fact, I believe he is entertaining serious thoughts of suicide," I said. "The events the night of Shelley's theatrical prove so."

"Poli? Ridiculous!" Albē replied. "It would disturb him far too grievously to know he could not attend his own funeral, dressed impeccably, and deliver his own eulogy! He put on a grand show that evening."

"We have been calling dangerous passions into play and none of us truly can know their final consequence—least of all for Polidori," I said quietly.

"Would you rather live in this world and call none of your passions into life?" Shelley asked. "I could not believe you could live that way."

Somehow his words ignited a spark within me and I felt anger rise. "No! But what a mart our world is! Feelings—those are our coin—and what is bought? Contempt? Destruction? Discontent?"

"A world few others have seen," Albē answered calmly.

I turned furiously on him. My anger had been building

slowly all these weeks as I saw Albé abuse Polidori and insult Claire, and deeper yet was my fury at Shelley for not speaking up, for not defending these weaker beings. "Well, my Lord," I said sharply and in a raised voice, "that makes the vast majority of mankind the unfortunate bastards!" I put my teacup down on the table by my chair and made to leave.

"Mary!" Shelley called, and as I began to walk from the room he immediately came to my side and took my arm to hold me back. "Mary . . . " he whispered low and reached for my shaking hand.

I could feel the tears rising, beginning to choke off my words. "I must be alone. For this moment, I pray you—I must be alone!" and I drew my hand from his and left him standing in the doorway, the firelight on his back. But as I entered my bedroom I saw him walk alone on the garden path outside leading to the lake.

I had not closed the bedroom door. Perhaps my true instinct had wished Shelley to follow me. I could hear Claire and Albé, and their voices sounded harsh. I went back to the door to secure it but could not help but pause and listen to their conversation.

"I have observed one thing in you that I like," Claire was saying. "Let a person depend on you, let them be utterly weak and defenseless, having no protection but yourself, and you infallibly grow fond of that person. How kind and gentle you are to children! How good tempered and considerate towards your servants! And all this because you are sole master and lord. Because there is no disputing your power, you become merciful and just. But let someone more on a par with yourself enter the room, you begin to suspect and be cautious and are very often cruel—as you are to me!"

"If I have been cruel, Claire, it has not been my intention."

Claire must have turned away, for her voice was now muffled. "I am sure that is so. Still, I will be glad that soon we shall be parted and I will not have to see your face and observe that impertinent way you have of looking at someone who loves you and telling them you are tired and wish they would go."

"I told you how it would be. I advised you against following me. I did everything to hinder you and now you complain of me!"

She walked away and closer to my bedroom door, and her voice was clearer and the pain in it more rending. "Do pray be kind to me, Albé. My one fear is lest you quite ignore and forget me. For, in spite of the bitter pain you cause me, I love you more and more each day."

Albé did not reply immediately and I closed the door between us and so heard no more.

> *We rest; a dream has power to poison sleep.*
> *We rise; one wand'ring thought pollutes the day.*
> *We feel, conceive, or reason; laugh or weep,*
> *Embrace fond woe, or cast our cares away;*
> *It is the same; for be it joy or sorrow,*
> *The path of its departure still is free.*
> *Man's yesterday may ne'er be like his morrow;*
> *Nought may endure but mutability!*

Shelley returned to the cottage and to our room late that night and only after I had spent the afternoon and evening in reverie and loneliness.

"Are you still disturbed?"

"No."

"And not angry I did not return?"

"No, it gave me time to think about my story."

"Mary?"

"Yes?"

"Would you prefer to sleep alone?"

"No. Oh, no!"

"I am pleased. This birth will mean as much to me as any child you bear me."

"You truly mean that?"

"Most reverently. You are all the woman I dreamed. Equal to any—man or woman." He touched my brow lightly with his lips. "When the time is come, I shall help, though the non-creator is always apart. It cannot be another way."

"You have created *this* Mary, so you are creator with me."

"You were this woman long before we met."

"Hold me, Shelley. The sky is filled with stars."

"I love you."

"And I love you and I still say you created this Mary."

He laughed softly. "If I have learned anything in this life, it is not to argue with a woman."

"Good night, Shelley."

"My darling—*good night.*"

How often do one's sensations change, and swift as the west wind drives the shadows of clouds across the sunny hill or the waving corn, so swift do sensations pass, painting—yet not disfiguring the serenity of the mind. It is then that life seems to weigh itself and hosts of memories and imaginations thrown into one scale un-

balance the other. You remember what you have felt, what you have dreamt, yet you dwell on the shadowy side, and lost hopes, and death, such as you have seen it, seem to cover all things with a funereal peace. The time that was, is, and will be *presses upon you, and, standing centre of a moving circle, you slide giddily as the world reels! You look to heaven and would demand of the everlasting stars that the thoughts and passions which are your life may be as everlasting as they. You would demand of the blue empyrean that your mind might be as clear as it, and that the tears which gather in your eyes might be the shower that would drain from its profoundest depths the springs of weakness and sorrow. But* where are the stars? Where the blue empyrean?

24

And thou, strange star! ascendant at my birth,
Which rained, they said kind influence on the earth,
So from great parents sprung, I dared to boast
Fortune my friend, till set, thy beams were lost
And thou, Inscrutable, by whose decree
Has burst this hideous storm of misery!
—MARY SHELLEY, *The Choice*

There is a portrait of my mother, painted by Opie, as
the frontpiece of one of her books. It is the only likeness I
have ever seen and I have studied the intelligent face in
that portrait a thousand times over and I believe I have it
so firmly in my mind that, could I but paint well, I could
duplicate it in perfect exactness. The dark eyes beneath
the naturally arched brows are turned to look at
something that has caught their attention. The glance is

:[221]:

misty, knowing, the softly curved mouth already smiling in tender delight, the expression on the smooth oval face can only be termed *womanly*. Gentle waves of dark hair nestle against the broad forehead and then gracefully sweep back to frame the face. The hair is shorter than was the style and unbound as is the body—draped in unadorned cloth in Grecian folds, the neck nude and the skin milky white. It is difficult to conceive that because this woman had the courage to express opinions new to her generation, and the independence to live according to her own standard of right and wrong, she was denounced, and the young were forbidden to read her books, and the more mature warned not to follow her example, and all the miseries she endured declared just retribution for her actions. Death did not moderate feelings against her. A sketch of her life in Chalmer's *Biographical Dictionary* perpetuated this ill-repute by treating her with scurrilous abuse, even in my generation. And my liaison with Shelley appeared to excite more public animosity towards *her* than myself. Little of her life or the opinions of the public were ever hidden from me. In fact, my father, once both Fanny and I were of an age to understand, felt impelled to convey to us both the full measure of our mother's suffering and of her remarkableness.

When my father met my mother, he was forty years old and at the height of his fame, and she thirty-seven and deemed the cleverest woman in England. Yet, both their works created scandal and evil talk. Few women have ever approached the depth of misery my mother fathomed. Born poor but middle-class, her education was hard-won and self-achieved. She was at an early age much alone. She lived many hard years serving in upper-class homes as a governess. She was quite often ill and when she turned to her literary work entirely, she existed in near poverty. Her fame did not bring fortune, but voices raised against her and doors slammed in her face. By the intellectuals she was, however, held in high esteem and her achievements brought her good friends among them. She lived in Paris as the terrors of the French Revolution grew greater each day and the English who remained in Paris ran the daily chance of being arrested with the priests and aristocrats and being carried to the guillotine. There she met an American, Captain Gilbert Imlay, who had taken an active part in the American rebellion and was an historian and author on his own. It was a violent attraction. My mother's convictions held that legal marriage was against the welfare of society. She had seen her mother lead a tortured life because the law would not permit her to leave a brutal husband. She had watched whilst her sister was driven mad by the ill-treatment of a man to whom she was bound by legal ties. Her view was, therefore, "that mutual affection was marriage, and that the marriage tie should not bind after the death of love, if love should die." And so she consented to live with Captain Imlay, if no religious or civil ceremony would sanction their union. It was not long before Fanny was born and, with the Revolution increasing in danger, that they moved to London.

But the fire of his love soon burnt out and no power my mother had could seem to rekindle it. Captain Imlay returned to Paris with another woman. My mother was broken-hearted. She wrote a note arranging for Fanny's care and then, with the calmness of despair, she hired a boat and rowed to Putney. It was a cold, foggy November day and by the time she arrived at her destination, the night had come, and the rain fell in torrents. She wet her clothes thoroughly before jumping from Putney bridge so that their weight would cause her to sink rapidly. She walked up and down the bridge in the driving rain, the fog enveloping the night in a gloom as impenetrable as that of her heart. Finally, she leapt, but she did not sink at once, only fainted. Moments later she was found floating on the surface, still alive. Once revived, her sense of survival appeared to rekindle itself.

It was not long after that that she met my father. Never in all her life had she needed sympathy as she did then, for she was virtually alone and caring for herself and Fanny, writing twelve, sometimes fourteen hours a day. For my father, who had lived a self-imposed and rather puritanical life until this time, his own world became revolutionized. They formed a union unblessed by clerk or clergy. Seven months passed and my mother found herself with child.

They were married at Old St. Pancras Church, where she is now buried. My father has often told me that my mother, due to her own experience, was unwilling to incur my exclusion from the society and could not in good conscience carry the burden of causing me grievous damage, and so in direct opposition to her beliefs married him. But until the moment of my birth, they lived apart as they had before. Only for the last twelve days of my mother's life did she cohabit with my father under one roof and then she was mainly unconscious.

My mind was awhirl with the first stirrings of my story and my mother's image—always as she is in the Opie portrait—had flashed like summer lightning through my clouded thoughts. When still girls, I would study Fanny's face and then my own. Which of us revealed ghostly glimmerings of our mother? Fanny had inherited the melancholy of *her* temperament which permitted no illusions, no moments even of respite from care in unreasoning gaiety. Yet, though full of warmth and of sympathetic nature, there was little else in Fanny to conjure up the woman in that portrait. Fanny saw things in the light of the commonest day, a fact which deepened her melancholy until her letters now alarmed me.

But I tried to put Fanny out of my mind.

The lady in the portrait. I concentrated on that memory.

When I sat, my glance turned just that way, I was surely *she*. I smiled and felt the likeness not needing a mirror to confirm it. There was my voice which my father reacted white-faced to at times, once saying—*I thought I heard Mary call*, and I knew he did not mean me.

My mother never held me. Perhaps that accounts for my inability to recall any sensation before I was three. I have a recurring dream and I dreamt it again only this last night. And in it I was birthed, a child already three, but born not by any human means. I was exhaled whole by a cloud of wind to stand upon a vast wasteland, alone, no living thing in sight. I woke, as always, as I searched endlessly, it seemed, for other life, a sense of desolation so painful in my heart that it took many hours to dislodge it from my being.

Shelley sensed my uneasiness and spent the day close by my side. We travelled into Geneva and bought a watch for Fanny, which I hoped would please her, and

:[225]:

shared an afternoon of great delight. We returned to Chapuis before the day had ended to find Albé waiting for us there.

"I thought we might go out on the lake," Albé suggested. But he directed the invitation to Shelley.

"May I go along?" I asked.

"Oh? I thought you might like some time away from Shelley," Albé said. "You appear to seek more and more private hours of late."

"Not today. I would, in fact, prefer not to be alone."

"Claire is in her room resting," Albé mentioned.

"Then I will see to her first and then join you on the dock."

Claire looked wan as though she had been weeping. She lay on a bank of pillows, her unbound hair cascading about her small face.

"Would you like me to remain here with you?" I asked.

"No. My bad dreams returned last night. I hardly closed my eyes. Perhaps I will sleep some before you return."

"If you are sure?"

She nodded, but took my hand and I sat down on the bed by her side.

"Do you think it is wrong to put an end to one's sorrow?" she sighed.

"Of course, it is! You must not think such thoughts!"

"The weather has been so dreary and nothing seems as it was. Nothing ever is, I suspect, but it has caused my mind to dwell on the most awful thoughts." She still held my hand tightly in hers but with the other I stroked her brow. "I often think of it when everything becomes so gloomy and desolate. But then I force myself not to think at all. It seems to me there is much madness in thought."

I managed a small laugh. "There is madness in all things."

She closed her eyes and I thought she might be asleep and began to ease my hand from her grasp, but she held firm and glanced up at me again. "We do torture ourselves so," she said softly. "Is it because pain reminds us so conclusively of our aliveness?"

"Perhaps. I never thought about it that way. But— perhaps—"

"I still love him. Madness, I know. But I do. And it is over for him—if, indeed, it ever truly *was. Clare* . . . " she laughed painfully. "I do believe that is why he gave me audience that first time. My name, though not spelled the same, brought back tender memories." She turned her head to the wall. "And still, I love him. I tell you it is madness." Slowly she forced her glance back to mine and breathed deeply and let go my hand. "I have always felt quite envious of you. I am rather small and weak that way. I would have given all I might possess for your romantic memory of your mother to take the place of the living reminder of mine. She is a terribly dull woman, rather waspish as well. There are times I wonder how your father bears her."

"He is your father, too."

"Not by blood, which is certainly evident!" Then she looked past me and to the window behind me. "He promised me, it is true, that my child whatever its sex should never be away from one of its parents while young. You and Shelley were both witness."

"The promise was not to give the child into a stranger's care until it was past seven."

"But you *will* bear witness?"

:[227]:

"Of course."

She sighed deeply. "I think it might storm."

The sky had turned dark but there appeared to be no wind. "I think not, but I shall stay with you, if you wish me to."

"No, please go." She lowered her lids with a small flutter. I stood and watched her until her breath was even and her lips parted loosely. The storm I feared that moment was not beyond the mountains, but a time not far away when we were returned to England and Claire's time was due. Her pledge to give up the babe would not be an easy one for her to keep and Shelley and I would be directly responsible to both mother *and* father.

"Perhaps it will storm," I said, as I stood by while Shelley and Albé readied the little boat.

"There is nothing that pleases me more than a boat ride in a summer storm!" Albé claimed.

"Would you prefer to remain here?" Shelley asked.

"No. I would rather be with you."

The storm clouds appeared to be in the distance beyond the far mountain, and Albé was an expert boatsman and I knew would hold a course not far from shore. The men steadied the boat while I climbed aboard and then they climbed in after me. Shelley seemed very happy and tranquil of mind. Albé sang as he directed the small craft away from our dock and out into Lake Leman. Twilight still hovered about us and in the grey-violet mist we could see Mont Blanc and the assemblage of mountains that vainly endeavoured to emulate her; and opposite, the mighty Jura, dark and giantlike, an insurmountable barrier to any invader.

The day grew closer to its end and the wind carried us effortlessly along and then gentled to a light breeze; the soft air just ruffled the water and we were still near enough to shore that it brought with it the delightful scent of flowers and hay. The men were engaged in a conversation about a guest of Albé's who had newly arrived in Geneva, Monk Lewis, an author of spectral horrors which held all his readers in a trance. I had met and found him more like a kindly English gentleman and, not truly meaning him a disservice, a bore. Albé, in his usual succinct manner, considered him "a jewel of a man, had he been better set." A West Indian property owner, he was aghast at the cruelties of the slave traffic conducted there and Shelley and Albé had entered with sympathetic zeal into his views. They had, in fact, just the day before witnessed an amazing codicil to Monk Lewis' will forbidding the sale of any Negro on his property or the diminution of any comforts or indulgences which he had allowed them whilst alive.

"I might reconsider my estimate of Monk Lewis," Albé was saying, "his characters in his books may all be sheetless phantoms made of air, but Monk is rather a man of good substance, I would say."

The light was soon gone and the lake and shore and mountains, though displaying their black outlines, were obscured. The moon was concealed behind dark patches of night and we made our way by the light of the boat's lantern. The wind, which had fallen in the south, now rose with great violence in the west.

"Perhaps we should head back," Shelley said.

"In time, in time," Albé replied.

I watched his face in the lantern's glow as he worked to

keep the boat on course. I had seen other men who re-
sembled him then—my father during passionate
debate—a messenger driving hell-bent across the
Scottish moors—Mr. Baxter in pursuit of the fox. Albé
was a driven man, delirious in his dedication and as I
never doubted my father's eventual victory in debate, or
the messenger arriving in time, or Mr. Baxter's out-
running the fox—neither did I doubt at that moment
that Albé would see the boat and us in it safe and shored.

There was the sound of thunder in the distance and
then rolling closer. We were now amid breaking waves
and a chaos of whirling foam. Shelley was at Albé's side,
working with the single sail.

"Let go," Albé shouted and, attempting to hold fast
his side as Shelley obeyed, very nearly catapulted over the
side. The boat pitched and Albé fought tenaciously with
the sail. For a moment the boat was caught under a wave
but was quickly brought to surface again. We were all
drenched. Both Shelley and Albé removed their jackets
and as one wave after another crashed into the boat, we
bailed the water out. Albé remained able to hold the sail
and for the moment the boat obeyed the helm.

"It will be behind us in a few minutes," Albé called.

The thunder was overhead and then lightning struck
not far away and in its brilliant flash the angry waters,
like a pack of mad dogs frothing at the mouth, rose
ferociously in huge dark humps. And then the rain came
down in torrents.

Albé, holding the sail with all his strength, turned his
face skyward and shouted at the top of his voice. "Blast
you! Blast you!"

"This is no time for a challenge!" Shelley shouted back.

I saw Albé's face distorted in laughter, but the storm was too violent to hear even the echo of his laugh.

It seems quite strange to me now but I experienced no fear but in its place a tremendous feeling of excitement. I could not swim and if I had been able, my skirt would certainly have drawn me under. Shelley could not swim, either, but Albé was expert and famous for his efforts. Thankfully, we were not too far from shore.

"Damnation! The rudder is broken!" Albé shouted.

There was no time for reply. The little boat spun dizzily around.

"Jump!" Shelley yelled at me.

"I cannot! It is impossible!"

The next moment, however, I was in the water and before I had time to panic, Albé had his arm about me and was swimming with me towards the shore. As we reached it, he let go of me and I pitched forward and into a bank of sodden mud. At that moment a wave came over my head, but I held fast and kept my face down and tucked in my folded arms. When the water pulled back, I dragged myself over and into a sitting position.

Near the shore the little boat was still spinning and pitching, deserted, without its captain and without Shelley. "Shelley!" I screamed and managed to pull myself to my feet. My dress was heavy with mud and the rain made it impossible for me to see. I drew back away from the water's wrath and walked leadenly along the shore. "Shelley! Albé!" I continued calling.

Then, suddenly, there they were! Or at least two forms

in the dense darkness who *must* be them. Both terror and thanksgiving drove me on—for the forms did not seem to move. And then one did—and raised itself above the other. I stumbled to their side.

Albé, breathing in desperate gasps, was kneeling over Shelley's inert form, his mouth touching his—breathing directly into Shelley's—desperately trying to impart his own breath into Shelley's lungs. I had seen nothing like it before. An incredible fight for Shelley's survival was raging within Albé.

The moments seemed endless and we were enveloped in the torrential rain. I understood that Shelley had somehow cleared our bobbing craft, that Albé had reached him and dragged him onto shore.

I fell down on my knees in the deep mud beside them and placed my hand on Shelley's pulse. It beat faintly and in a moment's time his chest began to rise slowly. Albé drew away. Shelley rolled his head and coughing and spewing, and vomiting, turned his face to one side.

Albé stumbled to his feet and between us we raised Shelley to his. There was a boathouse not far away and a lighted villa above it. We walked painfully with the full weight of Shelley between us, the rain slashing at us. At last we reached the boathouse and some shelter, and once inside, eased Shelley against a wall.

We were wet through and covered with mud. I feared for Shelley's condition. His breath was faint and his strength gone. I searched every corner of the boathouse and brought him whatever covering I found. Albé helped me remove Shelley's wet clothing. We replaced his boots with the worn, oversized old seaman's. Then we covered him with canvas and built a fire in an iron tub which we dragged to his side. Shelley was exhausted and he seemed to doze, though I feared he might have drifted into unconsciousness.

I was kneeling beside Shelley and Albé stood over us. I looked up at him in terror.

"He is only sleeping," he assured me.

I rested my ear against Shelley's chest. His breathing was eased but still faint. I sat back, aware for the first time since the boat had capsized of myself and of Albé as well. Until now all my concern had been for Shelley.

"You are soaked through," I said to Albé. I went to rise and he, seeing me waver, held his hand out to steady me. "It is my skirt," I smiled, "it is unbalancing me with its weight of wet cloth and mud." I moved away and towards the rear of the boathouse. "There was another pair of boots. Let me find them for you." I was rummaging through some store boxes.

"No!" he called to me, but I had found them and held them in my hand. "No!" he repeated vehemently.

"You can go to the rear to change," I said, understanding immediately. "It would be easier if you sat on that packing case, I will stay here with Shelley if that is all right?"

He grumbled and took the boots from my hand and moved towards the packing case.

Immediately, I turned my back to him and leant over Shelley.

I knew Albé's deformity was uppermost in his thoughts, and that it influenced every act of his life, that it had spurred him on to poetry as that was the path open to fame for him, and as if to be revenged on nature for sending him into the world "scarce half made up," he had therefore scoffed at her work and traditions with the pride of Lucifer! He was sensitive and not one of us ever dared pry into the cause of his lameness, nor did he ever expose his deformity to us. Claire had confided that he always unclothed in the dark and wore bed socks as well.

It was generally thought his halting gait originated in some defect of the right foot or ankle—the right foot was the one he dragged, and that it had been made worse in his boyhood by those vain efforts to set it right. I had heard that for several years he had worn steel splints, which so wrenched the sinews and tendons of his leg that they increased his lameness; the foot was twisted inwards, only the edge touched the ground, and that leg was shorter than the other. His shoes were peculiar—very high-heeled, with the soles uncommonly thick on the inside and pared thin on the outside. Claire said the toes were stuffed with cottonwool. He always wore his trousers very wide below the knee and strapped down so as to cover his feet. He entered a room with a sort of run as if he could not stop, then planted his best leg well forward, throwing back his body to keep his balance. I was aware, as well, of the pain his deformity often caused him, aware of the flush that rose in his face—the veins that swelled in his forehead, the quivering nerve on the side of his face.

I heard him struggling to remove his wet boots. Try as I could to stifle it, a morbid feeling was goading me to turn somehow and look at him and upon his deformity. But we had lighted several lanterns that we had found and with the fire beside me, I was afraid he would catch me at it. I glanced down to the ground and in so doing slowly shifted my glance to the side and back—*back* to the rear of the boathouse—to the ground before the packing case where he sat.

He was not putting on the boots but was, instead, tearing strips of rags and binding them around his feet— each one carefully, slowly. Then, painfully, he drew his own boots back over the bandages. He had been so absorbed that he had not seen me. I dared not look longer and turned my glance back to Shelley.

I felt revulsion! Yes! But more acutely I felt a pain that grew to such intensity within me that I thought I might faint. No pain I could suffer I knew that moment could, however, equal the pain Lord Byron had been made to bear since birth.

Both his feet were clubbed, one worse than the other, and his legs withered to the knee, again, one worse than the other. What a curse to chain such a proud and soaring spirit to the dull earth!

He was done. Slowly he dragged himself back to my side. I could not yet look up at him. My eyes were riveted upon his boots and I could not draw them away.

"I will go up to the main house," he said. I raised myself to my feet and nodded. Then he grinned with huge, almost salacious enjoyment. "Do you suppose the ladies will faint upon seeing the infamous Lord Byron appear, rain and mud-soaked, on their doorstep? They will probably believe I have, as they have always suspected I would, turned this very night into a muddied Devil who had burrowed his way out of the deep!"

I thought, *the form and features of an Apollo and the feet and legs of a satyr.*

He laughed and turned to go.

:[235]:

"Will you be all right?"

"Yes, yes," he replied impatiently. I watched him cross to the door. The added cloth inside his boots, though it protected and dried those feet, must also have been causing him great pain. He took some steps, paused, leant against a wall and then painfully continued on.

"Albé . . . " Shelley whispered and raised his head.

He turned and waited for Shelley to speak.

"I owe you . . . my life," Shelley said softly and with great effort.

"I will remember that," Albé replied and then, limping grotesquely, disappeared into the blackness beyond.

that time and yet we were more and more alone. It was not the best of all situations.

It did, however, give me more time to devote to the creation of my story. I had, since the time when Albé and I had been alone in Diodati's library, given it constant thought. Truth was, I could not shake my preoccupation with it. *Creation* was the word that made the burden heavy. For to write a story was one thing, to *create* it, quite another, and I knew this story of mine would and had to be—*created*. I could not think what it would be, but its seed had been planted. And though I would not share the truth with another, not even Shelley, in my heart I knew that if I be mother—Lord Byron be the father.

"*We are both monsters . . .* " he had said.

The words echoed endlessly in my head and there was unvoiced fear in my heart, a fear only a mother knows— Shall it be deformed? Shall it be sane?

If my preoccupation was with the creation of the story, my daily occupation was in setting myself down to write, as I had also done that unforgettable time in Albé's presence, my biography. Or rather, biographical notes, chronologically arranged—of my life. I did not know what use this would be, or if a use would ever be found for it, but it ordered my thinking and somehow seemed preface to the tale I would soon begin.

There were letters always to be written as well, and they took up a good deal of my time. Fanny's letters had been arriving daily and were of such a disturbing quality that I always set myself to reply immediately upon receipt.

London, 6th of August, 1816

DEAR MARY,

From your last letter I perceive you think I colour my statements. I assure you I do not and only write you the truth for I feel it is my duty. Papa is in poor spirits. He sees no one. He has very little money and the new novel is not an easy task. He cannot sleep at night and is, indeed, unwell. And I have not a *sou* of my own. I am not well; my mind always keeps my body in a fever; but never mind me.

I am much more interested in Lord Byron since I have read all his poems. When you left England, I had only read *Childe Harold* and his smaller poems. The pleasure I owe him for having cheered many gloomy hours makes me wish for a more finished portrait, both of his *mind* and *countenance*. From *Childe Harold*, I gained a very ill impression of him because I conceived it was *himself*, not withstanding the pains he took to tell us it was an imaginary being. *The Giaour, Lara,* and the *Corsair* make me justly style him a poet. Do, in your next, oblige me by telling me the minutest particulars of him, for it is from the *small things* that you learn most of character. Tell me if he has a pleasing voice, for that has a great charm with me. Does he come into your house in a careless, friendly, dropping-in manner? I wish to know, though not from idle curiosity whether he was capable of acting in the manner that the London scandal-mongers say he did. You must, by this time, know if he is a profligate in principle—

a man who, like Curran, gives himself unbounded liberty in all sorts of profligacy. I cannot think from his writings, that he can be such a *detestable being*. Do answer these questions for me, for where I love the poet, I should like to respect the man. As well, if you have any copies of his recent work written whilst in your company, please favour me with that and any recent poems of Shelley's, for I love to share, if only in that small part, some of what you are now experiencing.

Give my love to Claire; thank her for her letter. Give my love also to Shelley! Adieu, my dear sister. Let me entreat you to consider seriously all that I have said concerning your father. Yours, very affectionately.

FANNY

Chapuis, 14th August, 1816

DEAR FANNY,

Your letter grieved me, but let me assure you I have always accepted anything you have written or told me with the greatest seriousness. It will, perhaps, ease some responsibility from your shoulders and a weight from your heart to know that Shelley, Claire and I will be returning to England before this time next month and that Shelley has heard that he will receive some money shortly and has offered to help Father the best he can.

A great deal has happened here but revealing it in

a letter would be quite painful and impossible. I shall take you in my confidence immediately upon our return. At the same time, I will tell you all you wish to know about Lord Byron. But until then—no, I do not think him a *detestable being*—though I cannot say he is *not* profligate in principle. I can remind you that there are shades in all things and nothing is either black or white.

Shelley has written only two poems, "Mont Blanc" and "Hymn to Intellectual Beauty" whilst here (and of which you already have facsimiles). He has been much concerned with the theme of a longer poem that he has not yet begun, but which I believe shall be based in part upon the Prometheus legend.

I do include the following three lines he wrote the day before last, entitled "Home":

Dear Home, thou scene of earliest hopes and joys,
The least of which wronged Memory ever makes
Bitterer than all thine unremembered tears.

Claire sends you her love and Shelley sends his along with mine, dear Fanny. Do fight to keep your spirits up. You will not long be alone and I shall do the best I can to share your burden.

Adieu, dear sister! The days will shortly reunite us!

MARY

P.S. I have enclosed a sketch I have made of Lord Byron. You can see that I do not find him ill to look upon. Had I the ability, I would like to have shown the depth and torment in his eyes. But in truth, I am confident, no artist could set a true likeness of him on paper. To still Lord Byron in such a manner is to find oneself looking at a death mask. The living man is elsewhere. I am not sure, for that matter, that he is not a *living spirit*.

26

Did I request Thee, Maker, from my clay
To mould me man? Did I solicit Thee
From Darkness to promote me?
　　　　　　　　　—MILTON, *Paradise Lost*

"They say Dr. Darwin has preserved a piece of ver-
micelli in a glass case and that by some extraordinary
means it has begun to move with voluntary motion,"
Albé was saying.

It was evening and we were all gathered at Diodati,
save for Polidori who had travelled into Geneva which
was his wont more often than not these last weeks. The
day had been more fit for November than mid-August.
But then it had proved a wet, ungenial summer, with
incessant rain confining us indoors more often than not.
This evening was filled with moisture but the rain had

:[　245　[:

not yet come. I was a devout and silent listener as Shelley and Albé talked. Claire sat by the window, away from the fire, her hands busy with her needlework, her glance from time to time shifting to the men, but quickly away again, mute as I was but from her nervousness I thought, perhaps, preoccupied.

"That brings to mind the probability of the principle of life being discovered and communicated," Shelley said. He stood beside the fire, hands outstretched to its warmth. I was grievously concerned about him, for though at first he seemed in good health after his near-drowning, he was coughing once again and as the dampness in the air had become such an incessant thing, I had noted he found it difficult to warm himself through.

Albé rose excitedly to his feet and began to pace. "Perhaps a corpse could be reanimated; galvinism has given token of such things. Perhaps the component parts of a creature might be manufactured, brought together, and imbued with vital warmth!"

Across the room Claire shivered at the thought and bent her head more intently and with deeper concentration upon her handwork.

"What an achievement that should be!" Shelley exclaimed. Then his face took on a great sadness. "And what a disaster it could be if one could not also create mind and heart."

Albé paused and then went to stand by Shelley, both of them studying the flames before them. Albé's hands were thrust behind him and interlocked, his shoulders back, his feet apart. For an instant the curious idea crossed my mind that he looked at certain times like portraits I had seen of Napoleon Bonaparte—whom he spoke about often with a mixture of bitterness and reverence. He never forgave Bonaparte for abdicating his throne and yet never gave him up, either.

"And dreams?" he asked Shelley or the flames, I was not sure whom or which. And as he said it, I wondered about Bonaparte's dreams and if, after all, Albé's might not be likened to his, and his exile from his country as well.

"Most certainly—*dreams*—for what is man without *dreams*? A world without wind," Shelley replied.

Albé turned his back to the fire and away from Shelley. "My dreams always seem of the most disturbing sort. When I was a child, they were martial—then frustrated love, then . . . "—his glance darted upwards, to the ceiling. " . . . I woke from the most blood-curdling dream this morning! Such a dream! My blood is still chilled. In it my mother . . . *a corpse* . . . was trying to . . . *overtake me*. I wish to hell the dead would rest! Dreams!" He turned again to Shelley. "They are the despoilers of reality! I have commanded my mind to obliterate the memory of that dream, but I cannot! It has haunted me the entire day." He smiled thoughtfully. "I suppose one could accept the fact that the body works independently of the mind and so, therefore, the mind could work independently of the body as it does in dreams—madly and incoherently, I grant you—but still it is a mind and independent. One could speculate if the hypothesis could follow, that a mind could be transplanted from one body to another. Or a heart, for that matter!"

Claire shuddered and her needlework slipped to the floor, where she allowed it to remain. "I find all this talk most upsetting. Anyway, there are certain things that we must simply accept."

"Are you trying to say," Albé's mouth seemed set in a lion's jaw, "that man should not reason? You might as well tell man not to wake but sleep!"

"Please, your Lordship, *please* change the subject," Claire begged, appearing on the brink of tears.

"I am not your gaoler, Claire. You are free to leave."

She looked at him with great hurt but immediately got to her feet. "I shall do that, of course." She spoke with the edge of pride. She glanced hopefully at me and then away as she knelt to collect her embroidery.

"I will accompany Claire home," I said and went to join her at the door.

"I will not be responsible for disrupting your evening," she replied but with little conviction.

"I have a book to read and some notes to write and I am quite content in the anticipation of that," I assured her, "and Shelley can certainly remain. The weather may be damp but it is not yet wet. We shall see each other at home," I concluded.

I ushered her out as quickly as I could and reassured Shelley that there was little danger for two women on such a moonlit night and on a private path. Within moments I was on my way with Claire home to Chapuis.

My thoughts were crowded with the conversation Albé and Shelley had had. Claire walked silently beside me and I was thankful she did so for, in truth, she had not disrupted my evening but given me the excuse I dearly needed to leave Diodati and to contemplate what I had heard. I walked quickly, hardly feeling the dampness of the night or the ground beneath my feet. Claire, perhaps, believed me to be fearful of the darkness of the night and, hurrying to keep pace with me, entwined her arm through mine.

Upon arriving at Chapuis, I excused myself as soon as seemed politic and went directly to my room, sealing the door shut behind me. If these last few nights were any example, I could be certain that Shelley would not be here to join me before the first light of morning. This had disturbed me greatly, but curiously did not do so this night. I undressed without benefit of candle and paced the room in the misty moonlight glow. The midnight chimes rang out from Cologny before I placed my head upon my pillow. I could not sleep. My imagination, unbidden, possessed and guided me, giving the successive images that arose in my mind a vividness far beyond the usual bounds of reverie. I saw—with shut eyes, but acute mental vision—I saw a pale student of unhallowed arts kneeling beside the thing he had put together. I saw the hideous phantom of a man stretched out and then, on the working of some powerful engine, show signs of life and stir with an uneasy, half-vital motion. Frightful must it be, for supremely frightful would be the effect of any human endeavour to mock the stupendous mechanism of the Creator of the world. His success would terrify the artist; he would rush away from his odious handiwork, horror-stricken. He would hope that, left to itself, the slight spark of life which he had communicated would fade, that this thing which had received such imperfect animation would subside into dead matter. He would sleep; but be awakened; open his eyes and behold the horrid thing standing at his bedside, opening his curtains, and looking down on him with yellow, watery, but speculative eyes.

I opened mine with terror. The idea so possessed my mind that a thrill of fear ran through me, and I wished to exchange the ghostly images of my fancy for the realities around. I studied the room, the dark parquet, the closed shutters with the moonlight struggling through, and concentrated on the images I had of the glassy lake and white high Alps beyond. But, I could not so easily dismiss my hideous phantom; still it haunted me.

I had found my ghost story—my tiresome, unlucky ghost story. What had terrified me, I knew, would terrify the others. But for me, *I shivered as I thought about it*— was my dream, as Albé had said, *a despoiler of reality*? Or had it become reality itself?

The night waned and I passed it alone. No! That was not true, for my dream—my student—that . . . *that grotesque monster* never left me until dawn when Shelley's footsteps on the wet grass beneath the window, the gently opened but creaking door, the shadowed figure in the dim light, chased them finally away.

27

I awoke only short hours after I had fallen off to sleep with an immediate sense of excitement. It was true then! I had at last conceived my story!

The day was wet. The sky was dark. A storm appeared to approach rapidly. It was as though night had not lifted and I could hardly see the dark mountains. Fair preface to a story such as mine—a vast and dim scene of evil!

Shelley slept quite peacefully by my side. Cautiously, so as not to waken him, I rose and dressed in the gloomy dark, all but my shoes which I carried with me to another room and there stepped into them. Claire's door was shut and the servants were nowhere to be seen. I drew a cloak about myself and went out and stood beneath the protection of the entranceway. The rain came in large drops and its violence increased. Thunder burst with a terrific crash over the rooftop of the house. It was echoed over

Salève, Jura and the Alps of Savoy; whilst vivid flashes of lightning dazzled my eyes, illuminating the lake, making it appear like a vast sheet of fire. As is often the case in Switzerland, the storm appeared in various parts of the heavens at one time. I could see it dark and violent over Cologny, over the part of the lake which lies between the promontory of Belrive and the village of Copêt. Another storm illumined Jura with faint flashes, and another darkened and sometimes disclosed the Mole, a peaked mountain to the east of the lake. It was a wonderful sight! a noble war to behold! The wind was sharp and tipped with frenzied water and I felt lashed by an inexplicable excitement as it struck at me on the bare flesh of my forehead and cheek and hand—for the wind had shifted and the entranceway no longer afforded protection.

I went back inside the house and hastened to the library. A fire burned a welcome in the hearth. I lighted candles to dispel the gloom and sat down at Shelley's desk and began making a transcript of the grim terrors of my waking dreams. I had several pages filled before I paused—and I had only just begun. I knew the story I would tell would not only frighten but shock. I knew, also, that no matter how cleverly concealed, the personal nature of the tale I would unfold would not escape the sharpened senses of my companions. Yet, how could I truly explain? I felt a deep excitement at this thought. For, after all, was that not what Albé and Shelley had been seeking all summer long? *To exorcise our ghosts?* To expose the secret past we all lived so that there never more could be the fear to return?

I put my pen down and closed my writing tablet. I felt

like Scheherazade but unto only myself. I had bled enough ink for this day. This night would I continue.

I crossed to warm my hands at the fire and realized only then that in spite of the rawness elsewhere in the room, save by the fire, my palms were damp with sweat and my fingertips tingling with the fire heat of my own blood.

I rang the servant's bell for morning tea, though the clock in Cologny's spire told me it had just gone past noon, and then sat and waited for Shelley to rise to share the birth of my progeny with him.

I was quite prepared to tell my story that night, either at Chapuis or Diodati, but Albé insisted that we return to Chillon. It filled me once again with the same presentiments I always had when about to see that brooding castle and enter her neglected gates. In the end, I finally agreed because the others had not been granted exception and in fairness it seemed I should be a willing sport.

We set out early by coach. The roads were muddled into ditches by the storm and fallen rocks obstructed our path, and the way took longer than usual. Polidori had joined us this night. It was the first time I had seen him in over a week's time. He appeared gaunt, thinner, his face paler, his black hair, badly in need of trimming. He attempted to appear gay and in good spirits but I sensed that the effort weighed heavily upon him.

I had been relieved the past weeks at Polidori's defection because neither Shelley nor Albé seemed tempted to experiment with either laudanum or opium in his absence. I was, therefore, concerned to find he would

:[253]:

join us once more. But as we jogged along the rutted road, my apprehension eased. Polidori was neither glassy-eyed nor dreamlike and was not carrying his evil black satchel. He sat beside Albé, and I facing them, Claire on one side of me and Shelley on the other. Albé was in good humour and it spread itself to encompass Polidori. They exchanged bits of Geneva gossip (which Polidori was fond of relaying) and found a good many incidents to share their laughter. Shelley and Claire listened attentively and whenever Albé knew they were unfamiliar with the subject or object of their conversation, he would give them a further accounting. Whilst I . . .

. . . I leant back in the seat and rested my eyes and listened to the sound of the now soft rain upon the roof of the coach, and the dullness of the horses' hooves on the mired road.

I would tell the story first person, as if it were I who was engaged in this perilous experiment. And such it was for *I*—the *I* in my story, that is—would be a man of science who thought he had uncovered the principle of life. But before revealing it to the world, he must first experiment himself. He would spend his days and nights in vaults and charnel houses, beholding the corruption of death. He would study and examine all the minutiae of causation, as exemplified in the change of life to death, and death to life, until from the midst of darkness a sudden light would break.

This tale would not be the reveries of a madman. No! The *good scientist* would believe himself exactly that, and having discovered the cause of life, would dedicate himself to bestowing animation on lifeless matter.

He would collect bones from charnel houses and disturb with profane fingers the tremendous secrets of human frame. He would work in a cell at the top of his own house. He would put together a being of gigantic stature—perhaps eight feet tall, and endow this super-being with heart and mind and blood and sinew. And he would work, shunning the outside world until his creation would be complete and he could breathe into its unearthly tranquility the breath of life.

And then, because I had to have a name for this great scientist so as to add reality to my tale, I engaged, for the remainder of the journey, in the search for a suitable one. It was almost as we drew to the gates of Chillon before I had come to a decision. These stories had all begun because Albé had been reading a translation of some German volumes of ghost stories. My background would be the environs of the ride from Chillon to Geneva but the good Doctor would bear, because of his heredity, a German name. He would be from this moment forth—*Dr. Frankenstein.*

I had been so engrossed in my own thoughts that time had passed quickly indeed and given me no spare moments to ponder my fears at returning to Chillon. But as we ran from the coach, through the dark and damp night, Albé's loud encouragement sounded like angry shouts and Claire's laughter had the edge of a scream. I shivered as I followed behind them, and rushing to keep pace, arrived in the entranceway to the dungeons almost as they did. As everybody shook out their cloaks and wiped the rain from their faces, I turned and looked across the courtyard and searched the windows that circled it round. All was in darkness. Not another sound beside the rain and the gentle neighing of our horses could be heard. The castle appeared deserted with no evidence of Ianthe to be found.

We lighted candles and Albé led the way as we walked behind him single file down the stone stairs, across the small guard's room and into the dungeons. There were no moon, no stars, no outside light. Very cautiously we shuffled like some crawling serpent with flaming eyes along the hard cold stones, only able to see as far ahead as Albé's candle, and as far behind as the light from Shelley's, for as Shelley brought up the rear, he left a cavern of blackness behind us. Albé stopped at the Prisoner's Pillar and as we had done in most times past, we formed a circle. This time I was at the centre, before the Pillar. *His* chain rested quietly. The wind had died.

"Sit down," Albé said.

And we obeyed and placed the candles on the stones before us.

"Everyone touch hands," he whispered.

I reached for Shelley's, and Claire for mine.

My heart beat unmercifully. My hand trembled and Shelley pressed it gently to reassure me. I had told him the beginning of my story and he had been most enthusiastic and convinced me I should give even freer rein to my imagination and expand it. But still, my nerves did not calm. I felt, somehow, I was not alone in this experiment I was about to relate. Dead eyes, a stilled heart, a cold brow were somehow near and as I spoke of my creature's animation—I had this incredible presentiment—*I knew not what*—but my trembling never ceased.

And so, with the short preface I had created on the ride to Chillon, I began my tale:

"It was on a dreary night of November that I beheld the accomplishment of my toils. With an anxiety that almost amounted to agony, I collected the instruments of life around me, that I might infuse a spark of being into the lifeless thing that lay at my feet. It was already one in the morning, the rain pattered dismally against the panes, and my candle was nearly burnt out, when, by the glimmer of the half-extinguished light, I saw the dull yellow eye of the creature open; it breathed hard, and a convulsive motion agitated its limbs.

"How can I describe my emotions at this catastrophe, or how delineate the wretch whom with such infinite pains and care I had endeavoured to form? His limbs were in proportion, and I had selected his features as beautiful. Beautiful! Great God! His yellow skin scarcely covered the work of muscles and arteries beneath; his hair was of a lustrous black and flowing; his teeth of a pearly whiteness; but these luxuriances only formed a more horrid contrast with his watery eyes, that seemed almost of the same colour as the dun-white sockets in which they were set, his shrivelled complexion and straight black lips."

As I recited my story, I stared directly down into the candle's flame, not wanting to be distracted by anyone's glance, searching in the flame as though it were a mirror behind which my creation stared out and in moments I was transfixed, hypnotized as by my creature's eyes, and yet all the time aware that such was my state.

I heard the echo of my voice as I spoke and it rang terror in my pounding heart. My limbs ached as the good

Doctor's must have done as he ran from the sight of his creation and locked himself in his room. And I started in horror as though just awakened from a terrible sleep and a cold dew covered my forehead as the candle's flame, seeming to be the yellow light of the moon, illuminated the miserable monster I had created, breaking through a shuttered window.

And once again the echo of my words filled my head.

"He held up the curtain of the bed; and his eyes, if eyes they may be called, were fixed on me. His jaws opened; and he muttered some inarticulate sounds, while a grin wrinkled his cheeks. He might have spoken, but I did not hear; one hand stretched out, seeming to detain me, but I escaped and rushed downstairs. I took refuge in the courtyard belonging to the house which I inhabited, where I remained the rest of the night, walking up and down in the greatest agitation, listening attentively, catching and fearing each sound as if it were to announce the approach of the demoniacal corpse to which I had so miserably given life."

My hands no longer grasped life on either side of me. I was standing, though I could not recall rising to my feet, and my back was pressed against the stone pillar so hard that the Prisoner's chain cut into my flesh. An incredible thing had seemed to occur. No longer did I feel as Dr. Frankenstein, but—as that hideous monster. I felt the flesh of my arms and traced the structure of my face. But if I were *he*, how would my own touch know my distortion? It was my heart, my mind. I was that creature. I knew no doubt. The eyes that stared up at me from the circle at my feet were in terror of my very presence. I held onto the cold stone pillar and ran my hand along the length of chain just to feel the shape of other things beside myself. And then I drew back and behind the post. They went to stand and follow—perhaps pursue— and I disappeared into the concealing blackness of the rear of the dungeons. I felt myself borne away as if by waves and lost in darkness and distance.

Footsteps . . . *many* . . . *not mine* . . . approached as I clung to the darkness about me.

"Stop!" I shouted.

And there was silence once again. I breathed deeply and the pain caught in my chest. I was *he* and out there in the silent dark was *my Creator.*

"Did you think I could not feel pain or anguish, or agony, or remorse? You are my Creator. You infused me with the brain of a great philosopher, and with the heart of a *woman*. A heart fashioned to be susceptible of love. And yet . . . you made of me . . . a monster!"

I could feel the sobs wrack my body but I felt no tear upon my cheek.

"Where . . . where . . . " I called out, " . . . where is there sympathy for a monster? This creature with a woman's heart, designed not for love but for experiment, to prove your special thesis? A means but to your end?"

A candle's flame wavered before my eyes.

"Mary, Mary!" *Shelley's voice.* I knew it. I had not grown mad.

I shook my head in an attempt to clear it and Shelley's hand was on my arm. I did not shrink from his touch. It was warm, familiar, *welcomed*. I took the candle he held out to me, but needing a moment to pull myself together, I turned away with it, towards the rear wall of the dungeons where the gallows were raised.

Never shall the sight that met my eyes leave my memory no matter how intent I am on its banishment! For there hanging stiffly from the noose, her great black eyes vacant and unseeing, her body grotesque in death, her mouth agape, there . . . there hung the corpse of Ianthe.

28

Rain . . . drizzle . . . mist . . . fog. One more final week of it. But now it hardly mattered. I had not the heart nor strength of body to venture out. My days were filled with forebodings, my nights with sleeplessness. It was impossible for me to erase from my mind's eye the horrifying sight of Ianthe dangling, like some grotesque puppet, strings broken, discarded and left to hang. I could not speak of it to Shelley or to Claire, though I knew each was suffering over the catastrophe as severely as I. Shelley did insist I listen as he informed me that she was hung by her own hand and that the Governor had been to see Albé and begged him not to speak of the matter for fear of giving rise to the most lurid interpretations of the *poor, unfortunate woman's* death, and had assured him as well, that it had no bearing in any consequence to *his Lordship* or to his guests. The incident was to be immediately forgotten and it was not to be recorded in the official books. But I knew however long I lived, Ianthe's death would not go unrecorded. And that Albé and I forever shared a secret guilt, for could not I have pleaded more, and could not he have been less harsh?

I had never before known anyone to take his own life. It brought to my conscience the moral issues surrounding a suicide. Suicide was, after all, *murder*. And murder was an end result of a severe social disease or of madness. Perhaps it was the latter with Ianthe. I clung to that idea. For, if she had been mad enough to commit murder, I had been the only one of our company to spend time alone with her and had, for that matter, done so not very long before her act of violence. Had I not *sensed* the danger *for her*? Should I not have somehow attempted to restrain her from committing that violence? And why, *why* had I not gone to see her after Albé's visit to the Governor? Why had she committed such an act on the night of our return and in the dungeons for us to come upon? Hate, vengeance, had we truly imbued her so with that, or even been a willing contributor so as to give rise to such fearsome violence?

The questions spun like a paper boat in a whirlpool. I could not close my eyes for fear a new image would appear. I would see the dungeons, the gallows, *the noose*—a body bizarre in the violence of unnatural death—and *the face*—a face that was not Ianthe's—a face which I did not recognize yet I knew must be—could be *no other* than *Harriet's* face . . . for folds of luminous purple satin flashed in the candle's glow. It was a shocking premonition, one I wanted wholeheartedly to deny. But it persisted, holding me in the most painful jaws of agony.

I was happy, indeed, therefore, when the post at last brought Shelley word that he now had the resources for our return to England and that Mr. Peacock was doing as he had been bid and searching out a country cottage for us. Shelley was elated and even Claire, though fearful of the months before her and distracted by the parting it would surely mean with Albé, began to smile again.

The preparations for the move began and Chapuis was filled with daily activity. We planned to tour France briefly on our return—Fontainebleau, Versailles, Rouen—and I was delighted, for the trip to Switzerland through France had been fraught with too many anxieties to make it conducive to touring.

But in my secret heart there were—reservations. No matter how ungenial the weather had been, in spite of all, in the very face of the horror we had been audience to, here at Chapuis on the shore of Lake Leman, *here* Shelley had been my true husband. Whereas in England there was Harriet and my fearful premonitions and there was censure still, and I must, in the eyes of the law, return to the use of the name—*Godwin*. More than anything I had ever wanted in my life, I wanted to be *Mary Shelley* forevermore.

In the pall of creative energy caused by the terrifying end of our last night in Chillon, my story had been very nearly forgotten. Whilst we readied our baggage for the journey, however, Shelley brought it to my conscious attention once again.

"It should be subtitled *The Modern Prometheus,* for so it is," he said thoughtfully, then realizing he had taken me unaware, "your Frankenstein," he explained, "and his hapless monster. I have hardly been able to think of much else today. Frankenstein, your modern Prometheus, bears a strong resemblance to Milton's ruined Satan of *Paradise Lost*. But it is the monster—yes, *the monster*—that is the story's finest invention."

"*Invention*—yes, I suppose you could call it that."

"Do you recall the speech—*the plea* you uttered for and by him just before—"

"Yes," I interrupted hastily, not wanting to discuss *the other*—"Yes, of course."

"Are you considering the monster to be a totally literate creature, well-spoken and possessing intelligence?"

"Yes, I am."

"You will have to develop the idea at greater length. It is most original."

"I thought of it as a short tale."

"No. It is a novel. I am certain of it." He straightened from the work he had been bent over and smiled. "Perhaps this summer shall end with more than ghostly visions, after all."

That night we travelled to Diodati for the last time. A high wind blew. Trees tossed restlessly in the darkness. Shelley and I arrived together, Claire having gone up earlier in the afternoon. It was pitchy dark, but as we approached the villa the candles were just being lighted. A servant opened the door to us. Polidori was not at home and Albé, we were told, would join us shortly in the library.

We had to pass his room, however, to reach the library. The door stood ajar. There was a cup of tea on the table next to two pistols, several daggers, bullets and a Turkish scimitar. Albé's small bulldog slept on the threshold. Branches were beating against the window-panes and there was, once again, the sound of distant thunder.

Albé heard our footsteps and thrust the door open.

"God bless me, Shelley! Suppose there should be a God—it would seem well to stand in his graces this night! I will say my prayers and write to Murray in the morning to put in a touch concerning the blowing of the last trump!" He laughed and would have joined us in the corridor, but Claire had heard us enter as well and had come to greet us from the library.

Albé stept back into his room.

"Oh! Have I intruded?" Claire inquired.

"Damnably!" he replied.

Claire went quite pale but was in control of her emotions by the time Shelley had stept to her side. "I shall be gone tomorrow. I trust you will be satisfied then," she said and drew away from our protection and went and stood before the door to Albé's room, no more than an arm's length from him. "You will write to me?" she asked him.

"Yes, yes. Of course I will."

"And you will be kind in your letters?"

"I will make every effort."

"If I could but see the future," she smiled wistfully, "I would want to know your destiny above my own."

"Oh, well, one does not have to be clairvoyant, my dear. There are two things in my destiny."

"Yes?"

"A world to roam in and a home with Augusta."

"Mary and I will see Claire home," Shelley interrupted.

"No, no!" Albé said, "leave Mary here. You can return for her and we can have a last argument before you depart for holy England." He came out into the corridor then and took my hand. "Go on, Shelley. I shall be civilized for Mary's benefit. You need not worry that she has been left with a barbarian."

"I . . . " I lamely began.

"You will come into the library with me and we shall discuss the strange vagaries of destiny," he smiled and drew me away and down the corridor into the library.

"One day I shall look into your eyes and no longer see fear harboured there," he said quietly. He was very close to me and even so his words were so soft as almost to elude me.

"I fear not you, Albé."

"Yourself, then?"

"Perhaps."

"Leave Shelley. Come with me."

"You are surely mad." I turned my head but otherwise did not move.

"As I have said before. What do you know of madness? You only know of love and desire and pride. I could teach you much of madness. It might make both a woman and a poet of you."

"I love Shelley and he loves me. There can be no one else for either of us," I told him, now looking deeply into his eyes, unafraid for the first time in the entire summer to do so.

"Shelley has only two loves. And neither of them is

you. They are England and his poetry. And it is to England and to Englishmen that he shall always give his life and his love. I have tried to convince him of the sheer idiocy of his dedication. You, Mary, have attempted to compromise his love, diminishing it by protecting it. Both of us have failed. We will always fail. Shelley is an incorruptible man. A man possessed by genius. But, of course, we will both try on. Diehards, the two of us. Shelley shall continue to aspire like the eagle and we shall, in our singular anguish, try to clip his wings, but we will fail. I pray we shall fail."

He turned away from me then and left me as he went back and opened the door. "I will have Fletcher bring you some refreshments while you await Shelley's return. But think about it, Mary. I cannot in all faith promise you the part of my love that remains with Augusta, but I can assure you a very lively and rewarding time if your answer be *yes*."

Polidori came in then and at my request saw me home. We passed Shelley on the way and I pleaded concern for Claire. He seemed satisfied and continued on back to Diodati.

Claire was already in her bedroom. Polidori sat on a packing case looking somewhat like an underfed but nonetheless sleek black cat. We spoke of generalities. He wished me well and I him. He remained no longer than the space of ten minutes' time and then he hopped off the packing case and hurried to the door.

"There will be sun tomorrow," he said and then was gone as quickly as a cat might be expected to disappear. But Polidori was no longer the man I had feared so at the start of the summer. My fears were now *for* him, not of him. And in that last moment we shared I seemed to see a death's head for his face.

At nine the next morning we departed from Geneva. The sun shone brightly as we drove slowly by the lake. We would mount Jura and pass La Vattaz and Les Rousses before the day's end. It was Thursday the 29th of August. We were soon in the shadow of Jura. Behind us was the summer and beyond the great dark mountain, autumn, the turn of the season. Beautiful autumn. I smiled, but in my heart the melancholy grew and a chill caused me to draw my shawl tighter about me. Shelley took my hand and held it securely in his own.

I did not glance back, yet I knew that the summer, like all things haunted, might never truly pass and would remain forever in my memory.

Epilogue

Winter in losing thee has lost its all,
And will be doubly bare, and hour, and drear,
Its bleak winds whistling o'er the cold pinched ground
Which neither flower or grass will decorate.
And as my tears fall first, so shall the trees
Shed their changed leaves upon your six months tomb;
The clouded air will hide from Phoebe's eye
The dreadful change your absence operates.
Thus has black Pluto changed the reign of Jove,
He seizes half the Earth when he takes thee.
> —MARY SHELLEY, "Proserpine"

Six years later, on the 8th of July, 1822— the fatal 8th I shall always call it —I finished the journal which Shelley and I had once kept together. Shelley died by drowning off the coast of Italy only four weeks short of his twenty-ninth birthday and twelve weeks short of my twenty-sixth. Albé had been correct. We did all meet on another adventure. It might aptly be called a rendezvous with death. England had not welcomed us home with open arms and my very worst premonitions became reality.

Less than a month after our return, my sister Fanny committed suicide by taking an overdose of laudanum. Two months later, Harriet drowned herself in the Serpentine (poor dead Harriet, to whose fate I owe my name and yet attribute so many of my sorrows) and six months after that, Polidori took his life.

England was grey and filled with bitter memory, and so once more we left her shores to join Lord Byron, this time in Italy.

But Shelley kept his vow. Never before had his work so consumed him. He wrote, it seemed, without pause, seldom remembering to eat, often refusing to sleep, spending a good portion of his days alone, and his work was, indeed, dedicated to England and to Englishmen.

I do not know how Shelley died. Or why the boat sank. Or why he could not reach shore. He had gone on a boating trip with a friend, Edward Williams, the curate who had married Harriet and Shelley and who with his wife, Jane, had been sharing a house with us by the sea. Neither Lord Byron, myself, nor Jane had accompanied them on this fatal excursion.

There had been a small squall but the boat had been well built. There was talk that they were attacked by Italian sailors in the hope they had much money on them. I never once conjectured. Shelley was dead, Edward Williams with him. How, never seemed to matter. Ten days later my own dear love was finally cast ashore.

The parts of his body not protected were fleshless. In his jacket was a volume of Sophocles in one pocket and Keats' poems in the other, doubled back at a passage of "The Eve of St. Agnes," as if the reader, in the act of reading, had hastily thrust it away. There was no doubt that this be Shelley.

The passage marked by Shelley's last living gesture was this:

Beyond a mortal man impassion'd far
At those voluptuous accents, he arose,
Ethereal, flush'd, and like a throbbing star
Seen mid the sapphire heaven's deep repose;
Into her dream he melted, as the rose
Blendeth its odour with the violet,
Solution sweet: meantime the forest-wind blows
Like Love's Alarum pattering the sharp sleet
Against the window-panes; St. Agnes' moon hath set.

We were forbidden by quarantine law to move or bury him elsewhere. And so he lay for many days longer in a shallow grave on a beach near the Gulf of Spezia. The decision was to incinerate his body where it lay and bury the ashes wherever I wished. I could not attend this first service, may God and Shelley forgive me. Lord Byron went in my place along with Leigh Hunt, Mr. Trelawny and a Mr. Shenley, who kindly brought me back the following report:

The body lay eighteen paces from the breaking surf. The sea, with the islands of Gorgona, Capraja and Elba, was before us, old battlemented watchtowers stretched along the coast, backed by the marble-crested Apennines, glistening in the sun, and not a human dwelling in sight. Mr. Shelley was moved from his shallow resting place, and the funeral pyre laid. Lord Byron set fire to it. But the body was slowly consumed and he turned away, unable to see more. The day was one of wide autumnal calm and beauty. The Mediterranean kissed the shore as if to make peace with it, and the flame of the fire bore away towards heaven in vigorous amplitude, wavering and quivering, a brightness of inconceivable beauty. During the whole funeral ceremony, a solitary sea-bird crossing and recrossing the pyre was the only intruder. Mr. Trelawny, at your request and entreaty, did preserve Mr. Shelley's heart. Lord Byron covered it with his own silk shirt and I, along with this account, do now hand it over to you.

Your heart—I have kept it all these years, never far from me.

I cannot grieve for you, dearest Shelley; I grieve for our friends—for the world—for myself; the glory of the dream is gone. I am a cloud from which the light of sunset has passed. *Meum cordium cor!* Good night! And in your own words:

"I would give
All that I am to be as thou now art;
But I am chain'd to time, and cannot thence depart."
> Mary Shelley . . . *forevermore.*

Postscript

The author would like to make special reference to the fact that various passages from her other works and from later reflections in her journal seem to appear in this work, and begs the reader's indulgence. For as Lord Byron said—*writers are the worst plagiarists*. And I must add to that *most especially of their own writings*.

M. S.

Author's Note

I am, and have always been, an incurable romantic, feminist and amateur detective. It was no surprise then that, in the course of my early reading, Mary Wollstonecraft Godwin Shelley should both fascinate and haunt me. Here was a woman who by the age of nineteen, not only challenged the mores of England, but changed the course of Shelley's life, fascinated Byron, and wrote the greatest horror masterpiece of all times—*Frankenstein*.

I set about reading all I could discover about Mary, her background and her associates. With great difficulty I managed to read all her work—not because it was so unreadable, for it was far from that but because it was so inaccessible. Mary's work except for *Frankenstein* and *The Last Man*, had not been reprinted since her lifetime.

My search for Mary's writings led me to the British

Museum, where the staff was extremely kind to me and allowed me to Xerox a great deal of her work so that I could claim it as part of my own library and reread it at my leisure. I did the same with the truly definitive biography of Mary written in 1889 by Mrs. Julian Marshall. This led me to study the complete notes of both Mary and Shelley in the first edition of *The Poetical Works of P. B. Shelley* edited by Mary herself. Mary spent most of the years after Shelley's death attempting to persuade Sir Timothy, Shelley's father, to grant her permission to write a biography of his son. Sir Timothy never relented in his refusal. To circumvent this obstacle and not lose Sir Timothy's support for herself and for Shelley's son, Mary, in the form of notes to Shelley's poems, managed to write a continuing biography of sorts. These notes were indispensable in my journey into Mary Shelley's life. So were her letters, her journal and the letters and journals of her contemporaries.

A picture emerged—mysterious and dynamic, and as filled with genuine horror, passion and complexity as the unnamed monster in *Frankenstein*, and yet as timely as any book one might find on the best-selling nonfiction booklist today. Mary was the daughter of Mary Wollstonecraft—author of *Vindication of the Rights of Woman*, advocate of free love. Mary was also William Godwin's daughter—Godwin, who was the political hero of the true revolutionaries of the late eighteenth and early nineteenth centuries, Godwin who wrote the great *Political Justice* and who had as his disciples all the young revolutionary minds of his time, including Percy Bysshe Shelley. Mary was Shelley's mistress while he was married and after Harriet Shelley committed suicide, his wife. She was the friend of most of the great young writers of her day.

There is little doubt in my mind that Mary was responsible for Shelley's early publication after his death. He had until his meeting with Mary been better known in England as a pamphleteer. She was dedicated to his success from the start, whereas Shelley was dedicated only to his writing. Though widowed at an incredibly young age, she chose to remain Mary Shelley for the rest of her years rather than encourage admirers such as Trelawny and Washington Irving. She never allowed the world to forget that she was *Mrs.* Percy Bysshe Shelley, and so completely did she succeed that she remains remembered in that fashion to this day. Few truly know who wrote *Frankenstein*. Few know the circumstances of its creation. And most believe it was conceived in all its horror as a late-night picture show. Reading it, after my study of Mary, I recognized the tremendous daring it required to write such a book in those times and the courage it took to reveal so much of a personal nature to a world that was already alien to her. For *Frankenstein* is of an extremely autobiographical nature. (As was *The Last Man*.) The characters are based on herself, on Shelley, and Byron, and Godwin, and Claire, Trelawny and Coleridge—all seen through Mary's unique eyes and given her bizarre interpretation.

I owe a great deal to the British Museum, to all those biographers and biographies that helped me piece together my story. I am deeply indebted to Mary's own work and her journal and her letters, to Dowden and to Hogg for their fine biographies of Shelley. I am grateful for the insights that came from Byron's journal and letters, from his work and the many biographies of him. I could not have evoked Chillon at all had it not been for the kindness and cooperation of the custodians of Chillon Castle. But most of all, I owe great thanks to the encouragement of my dear friend, Vera Caspary, the uncomplaining aid of another dear friend, Mr. Jay Schlein, and the assistance of my daughter, Catherine Edwards.

Beaulieu S/Mer
1972

ANNE EDWARDS